La Bayadère

Manon

Don Quixote

The Firebird

Starring Prima!
The Mouse of the Ballet Jolie

JACQUELYN MITCHARD

Starring Prima!

The Mouse of the Ballet Jolie

illustrations by
Tricia Tusa

HARPERCOLLINS*PUBLISHERS*

Library of Congress Cataloging-in-Publication Data
Mitchard, Jacquelyn.
   Starring Prima! : the mouse of the Ballet Jolie / by Jacquelyn
Mitchard ; illustrated by Tricia Tusa.—1st ed.
      p.   cm.
   Summary: In the old grand piano at the Ballet Jolie in New York
City lives a ballet dancer who just happens to be a mouse, and who
intends to become principal dancer in ballets for mice and humans,
and the occasional creature, as well.
   ISBN 0-06-057356-2 — ISBN 0-06-057357-0 (lib. bdg.)
   [1. Mice—Fiction. 2. Ballet dancing—Fiction. 3. Human-animal
relationships—Fiction. 4. Theaters—Fiction.] I. Tusa, Tricia, ill.
II. Title.
PZ7.M6848St 2004   2003014958
[Fic]—dc22   CIP
                                                 AC

Typography by Nicole de las Heras
1 2 3 4 5 6 7 8 9 10

First Edition

For my theater children,
best love from "Mama C."
—J. M.

Starring Prima!
The Mouse of the Ballet Jolie

A Star Is Born

ASK ANYONE WHO knows beans about apple butter. It's usually just no big deal when a mouse is born.

It happens every second, you know. Why, there are about two thousand mice for every human on earth. When you're walking along the street in the city, you might not know it, but you're never more than six feet away from a mouse. And though mice are very good parents, they try not to get terribly attached to their children, because those children grow up so fast that, before their mamas and papas know it, they're setting out to raise their own families. And once those kids start raising their own families, it's rare that their parents even get a paws-card!

But once in a while, along comes a mouse who may change the world—the mouse world, that is, a world human people don't think about very much until they call the . . . well, the pest control folks.

Just such a mouse was born one dreamy, snowy Valentine's Day morning in a cozy nest under the lid of an old grand piano at the Ballet Jolie in New York City.

She was one of a very special breed of mice, different from all the other mice in the world.

She was one of the artists.

Now, you've seen the work of the mouse painters, those who work in mixed media such as mud, cereal, snow, and peanut butter.

You know of the singing mice, such as Squeequido Domingo and James Tailer. There are the mouse authors, such as John Silverback, who wrote *Of Mice and Rats*, and of course, the famous German sable coat, Grimmouse, who wrote the nursery favorite

Whiskerella. (Well, yes, of course it was a mouse! If you've ever had a mouse nibble your Halloween jack-o'-lantern, you know that whoever thought up turning a pumpkin into a beautiful coach had to be a mouse, *not* a human.)

Mouse artists have brighter eyes and glossier coats, as well as more protective and doting parents. They don't learn to *scurry*; they learn to *stroll*. They crawl tall. French or Japanese or Italian or American, they know who they are, and they are quietly proud of it.

Because of their natural speed and instinctive prowess at all sorts of jumps, among the most extraordinary of the mouse artists are the dancers. And the newborn baby girl was one of these.

All mice are born with the ability to jump. However, popping out from under a pile of leaves is a long way from a ballet move such as a *grand jeté*. Not every mouse can make the leap. There's ever so much hard work involved, including hours of stretching and kicking while all the other mice are playing Freeze Mouse or Kick the Kibble.

Luckily the mice of the Ballet Jolie took their

heritage seriously, and when that baby girl was born, though she was the last and tiniest of the litter, every-one sensed she was something special. Before she went to sleep on the night she was born, looking no more obviously unusual than a little pink shrimp, she spoke. She murmured softly, "I am born to dance."

Her dear mama was so surprised that she almost rolled over on the rest of the babies, who all peeped in protest. And wise mother that she was, she quickly sensed that a whole new era was about to begin at the Ballet Jolie.

Bred for the Ballet

FOR A GENERATION Madame Mousielle had lived in peace and harmony with her growing family in the great auditorium of the Ballet Jolie. Her legendary journey across the ocean was well known among ballet-loving mice (and, given their propensity to run and jump, practically every mouse *does* love ballet). Despite their grand surroundings, Madame Mousielle's three mouse daughters were very good and obedient, and taught lessons with their *maman*. The eldest daughter was called Maria Tailchief, after her favorite American dancer, whom she'd heard of many times in her mother's stories. The next eldest, who loved modern dance, was called Twyla Tweek. And the third, a great fan of classical music (and an even greater fan of yummy treats), was called Pattypaw. In the theater called the Ballet Jolie, they had found a superlative home.

Now, if you've ever seen it, and maybe you have, you know that the Ballet Jolie is a mouse paradise, filled with thousands of nooks and a few dozen crannies as well. There are hand-painted golden banisters and filigreed sconces (with real wax candles!) for mice to gnaw upon, and beautiful velvet seats to tear apart to get to that luscious foamy stuff that makes a cozy mouse nest.

There is also a costume shop, filled with billowy tutus and soft, warm ballet shoes to curl up inside for naps, and best of all, a huge concession area where excited human children and happy adults are always dropping crumbs of delicate truffle cake, bits of chocolate wafers, and whole *handfuls* of popcorn. (To be quite honest, the mouse people sometimes influence humans to toss their popcorn with a little move called the dive and dodge. It is a precision drill, performed by four mice running in four different directions at once, meant to be glimpsed only out of the corner of an eye. It makes humans jump because they imagine they *might* have seen a mouse, though they're never entirely sure and usually feel quite silly and embarrassed afterward about having made a mess. Human adults are easily abashed. Human children usually see the whole thing clearly, but they get a kick out of it.)

When all of Madame Mousielle's daughters got married one romantic Christmas Eve, they naturally moved to their own "apartments" but remained at the Ballet Jolie.

The first daughter and her husband took as their family name Pianissima, because they lived backstage under the lid of an old grand piano that had been broken as long as anyone could remember.

The second daughter and her husband were known as the Mezzaninas. They lived in a cozy hole they enlarged in one of the ancient velvet seats so high up in the theater, hardly anyone ever used it.

And the third daughter, the one with the chubby

round tummy, became after her marriage Mrs. Snacketta. The Snackettas made their home in the wall behind the concession stand. They were always putting their children on diets, because the young mice ate so many gumdrops, popcorn kernels, and chocolate crumbs that they could barely fit through the cubbyhole of their house in the beautiful gilded wood of the baseboard.

After her daughters' marriages, Madame Mousielle rarely left the ornate canopy over the VIP box at the Ballet Jolie, where she had established a home for her young family after her ocean crossing in the white satin trunk of Renata Rousseau, principal dancer of the Ballet Français Minuscule.

Madame Mousielle's story was tragic. In her youth she had married an equally gifted dancer, Mousieur René Mousielle, who had the misfortune of being caught napping in a toe shoe when it was pulled onto the foot of a dancer who had to make a costume change in a great hurry.

The brave widow could not bear the grief of living at the Ballet Français Minuscule, where she had shared a life of love and art with her René. So, wrapping herself in a shawl of warm velvet, she stowed away for the long voyage to America, and one storm-tossed night on shipboard, she gave birth to six daughters. To amuse her babies through the long days and nights, Madame told tales of the sky-high buildings and the all-night music of voices and traffic that awaited them in New York City.

Three of the babies turned out to be little imps. Their trunk had only just been delivered to the Ballet Jolie when they headed to the streets in search of the high life. Bewitched by all the new smells and sounds in the big city, they ran away with handsome hoodlum mice as soon as they had learned the razzle-dazzle language of New York.

Still, her head high, Madame took up residence in the VIP box at the Ballet Jolie with her three remaining children. She taught them ballet, and they became mouse dancers of renown, their classical training bringing something special to their part of the city (mouse influence rarely extends beyond a few blocks, because their legs are so short). The Mousielles supported themselves with midnight performances, working for peanuts (literally) until Madame was able to find a large piece of broken looking glass and an iron doorstop for a ballet *barre*. She immediately set up a classroom behind the wall of the VIP box and welcomed the first paying students to her American Ballet Rodente.

Mouse mothers from as far away as Carnegie Hall and the basement at Bloomingdale's sent their children, boys and girls, to study with the stern but kindly Madame Mousielle. Under her tutelage Fred Moustaire learned the suave steps that made him a sensation in nightclubs under the best cement stoops. When the society mice, who lived in the great stone penthouses, learned that there was a Parisian ballet mistress teaching in New York, they sent their children too. The peanuts began rolling in—along with Brie, Camembert, and the occasional morsel of éclair.

Madame Mousielle attributed her strength and supple figure to the discipline of the dance and still did her exercises each morning at one A.M., even after her daughters were grown.

And that was just what she was doing when Mother Pianissima began grooming and admiring her own first litter of six babes—three girls and three boys. As custom dictated, Mother had waited until her babies got their first coat of soft fur before inviting visitors to inspect them.

Mother noticed that Mousie Child Six (who had yet to be named Prima) did not look at all like her sweet gray siblings. She was slightly darker, like a summer rain cloud, the color of the shadow makeup the principal dancers wore around their great, soulful eyes. She had exceptionally long legs, and pink paws as delicate as the sugar roses on a birthday cake.

Though in her day Mother Pianissima had been a fine dancer and performed many principal roles with her mother's American Ballet Rodente, she suspected that her smallest daughter, so precocious and beautifully formed, might be one of those ballerina mice who are born only once in a generation.

Mother Pianissima thought *perhaps* that Mousie Child Six might be the equal of her exquisite French grandparents, and *perhaps* might be celebrated not only about New York, but beyond. She thought *perhaps* her daughter might lead one of those traveling mouse dancer troupes who travel to far-off places (such as New Jersey!)—stowing away in the jump seats of rock stars' limousines, their costumes carefully folded inside sandwich bags, giving performances in the dressing rooms of great civic centers and amphitheaters.

Suspecting such a wonder, Mother Pianissima decided to take a serious step. She decided to ask her mother to make the long, unaccustomed journey down from the VIP box to make a special judgment about the new mouselet backstage.

She sent a paw print on a ticket stub, the traditional mouse sign for "alert," with a Snacketta nephew, who ran up the three flights to Mother Mezzanina, who sent her son Dusty up three more flights to the box-seat home of Madame.

"Grandmamma!" he cried. "Come and see the special baby!"

Though still spry, Madame Mousielle was past the days when she could leap down six flights with a few bounds. But she grasped her cane—a gold toothpick that had been dropped one night by a rotund millionaire struggling to get into his cashmere coat—and started down to the piano. The walk took her a full hour. When she arrived, Mousie Child Six was asleep beside all her siblings.

But Madame clasped her hands in rapture nonetheless.

"Merveilleuse! Charmante!" she whispered to her happy daughter. "She is the very picture of *mon cher* René!"

How Ya Gonna
Keep 'Em Down on the Farm?

THERE ARE TWO sides of the story of the mouse families of the Ballet Jolie. The reason that these families were so special wasn't entirely because of the grace and talent of their exquisite little gray mothers.

They had some hardier genes in their background as well.

Just as the mouse mothers were sisters, all the mouse fathers were brothers. And they were no ordinary brothers. Not by a long shot. In their own way, they were mouse artists of an unusual sort, and quite as accomplished as their wives.

They were Trappers, and not only were they Trappers, they were the very ones who had invented the Mousetrap Defeater, a helmet that could protect a relatively quick-pawed mouse from any trap, making it possible to snatch the cheese or, even better, the peanut butter. The Trappers had created the Mousetrap Defeater with the help of their father, old Moss Mouse of Littleton, New Jersey. It was made from the caps of Dee Lite Beer, which they found strewn all over after a rousing Saturday-night dance at the barn where they lived. Bent just the right way to fit the head of the individual mouse, the cap worked like a charm. Bartering the helmets had made the brothers Trapper a tidy little nest egg, which included a great many fresh eggs, along with nuts, crackers, and the stocking caps that mice love to use as sleeping bags.

The brothers met the sisters when their humans came to New York in a big farm truck to see *The Nutcracker* on Christmas Eve. The brothers had been under a hay bale, nibbling some leather boots in the back of the truck, at the time the family took off, and

so they went along for the ride. When the human family set off for the theater, the brothers simply hitched a ride in the farmer's broad-brimmed black Sunday hat. When the human family took their seats, the brothers went exploring. (A mouse can pretty much choose to be seen or not to be seen, depending on whether or not he feels like blending in or giving some human a start.)

It was love at first sight.

It wasn't that country mouse girls weren't pretty. The Trappers had sisters both strong and fair, including Milka, who had mastered the skill of leaping up and pulling on the udders of Patience, the cow, to bring home a nice bottle cap full of warm milk for Mother.

The Trapper brothers fell in love with the dainty ballet sisters simply because they had never seen mice so small of paw and sweet of face. They'd never even met a mouse woman who wore lipstick, which, of course, the theater sisters wore regularly in tiny mouse dablets. (They made up their own little makeup kits from matchbooks.) They also wore dabs of eye shadow and rouge they gently borrowed from the dressing rooms, and ribbons they removed from the ruffles of the dresses of certain leading ladies.

No wonder the brothers were bedazzled.

Yet it was more than mere romance.

It turned out that the rough-and-ready Trapper brothers loved everything about ballet—the leaps, the lights, the applause. *The Nutcracker* was a special stunner, given the Mouse King with all the swords and his seven heads. Though the Mouse King was a villain, the brothers could not help being intrigued by him. They could not imagine how a full-grown mouse with *seven* heads and *seven* swords could lose any battle.

"On the other hand, I'd like to see him try to take us on with our patented Defeater helmets," one brother said to another.

"What a wimp," another agreed. "Wouldn't last a week in Littleton. Why, I could've whipped that king with one head tied behind my back." (He'd made sure that the most beautiful Maria Tailchief was standing nearby when he made this boast.)

All the brothers did, however, think the Prince was

a right sort of guy, for a human, and were happy he got the girl in the end.

But so did the Trapper brothers!

One by one, that Christmas Eve, each Trapper brother took Madame aside under the holiday wreaths that glittered with miniature electric icicles. Each of them asked Madame for one of her daughters' paws in marriage.

One of the stage-door mice, who was always willing to run an errand for a pretzel, took off to fetch the Reverend Mousenior Patrick All'Ears, who'd been asleep after the long night's festivities in his mansion under the altar at Saint Patrick's Cathedral. Quickly the Mousenior carried a candle stub back to the theater, and the solemn ceremony was performed. Maria Tailchief and the eldest Trapper brother became the Pianissimas—because Maria had always had her eye on that old but still grand piano. The second brother happily married Twyla Tweek, and they became the Mezzaninas. Lovely, round Pattypaw became the wife of the third and youngest Trapper brother, and they chose the family name Snacketta. The newlywed couples spent the night settling into their new homes.

The human farm family went home three mice lighter, but who notices the shortage of three mice on a farm? The Trapper boys were good sons, though, and they sent word to their sister Milka and their parents with a farm rat who could speak both Mouse and Human. (Yes, it is true: Rats *are* smarter than mice, and even smarter than some people, though hardly ever as beautiful!) He'd spent the evening ignoring the ballet and searching nearby Dumpsters for delicious treats, but was more than happy to memorize a message before falling asleep in the bed of the pickup truck with his hands folded over his plump belly.

The Trapper brothers quickly took to city life. For one thing, the chance to see *The Nutcracker* twenty times every year was a terrific reason to give up the rugged, outdoor freedom of the farm, and the Ballet Jolie was much, much warmer than the milking barn when the cold winds blew, and ever so much cooler in summer heat!

But best of all, they loved the fact that there were so many mousetraps.

What a challenge!

Of course, the human people who worked at the Ballet Jolie *knew* there were mouse people around. And they did set traps, though many of them secretly hoped never to find a mouse in one! Angelo was the most kindhearted usher of all—such a child at heart that he still sometimes thought he could understand the mice talking, as all kids are able to do. Angelo actually sprang the traps the minute he set them.

Still, even Angelo had to put up at least a show of a battle against the resident mice. There was that famous night when one of the little Mezzaninas fell asleep in a rich lady's fur hat during the ballet *Mayerling* ("You could hardly blame the poor darling," Mother Mezzanina said later). When the lady picked up her fur hat, she screamed so loudly, everyone thought the screaming was part of the tragic show!

And so began the happy, peaceful lives of the Pianissima, Mezzanina, and Snacketta mouse families at the Ballet Jolie.

Life was peaceful, that is, until Prima came along.

On Your Toes, Mama and Papa!

VERY SOON ALL three young mouse couples became mamas and papas. And like all new parents they were very excited when the big day came and their babies opened their eyes. As you all know, mice choose their own names on the day that they open their eyes, and all little mouselets in a litter open their eyes for the first time on different days over a period of several weeks.

But before they open their eyes, they open their ears and listen. They listen for the name that will suit them best.

The largest and heartiest of Prima's brothers opened his eyes during the ballet *Cinderella*, and naturally enough, he chose the name Prince Charmant. The next brother opened his eyes during the same ballet and decided he would be called Cinderella.

"No son of mine is going to be named Cinderella!" Father Pianissima thundered. Mother Pianissima, always the peacemaker, quietly suggested that the beautiful name of the composer of the ballet, Prokofiev, might be best after all. And so Prokofiev he was.

Next born was round-bellied little Pan, the smallest of the brothers, who had a habit of laughing in his sleep and was as merry as the jolly forest god after whom he was named. Prima's biggest sister named herself in honor of her favorite ballerina, the great Pavlova. And her tallest sister chose the name Paris, also to honor Madame. ("I don't know if that's a very nice name for a girl," Mother worried aloud. "Better than Cinderella for a boy!" Father grumbled.)

Several days later, when Mousie Child Six finally and luxuriously opened her eyes, to her parents' eager anticipation, there was a legendary dancer onstage in a terribly sad and haunting ballet.

It was called *Anna Karenina*, the story of a beautiful, foolish woman who throws her love away upon a cruel and handsome man whose heart is a shard of ice. The woman who played Anna was named Antoinette Brown, and she was the principal dancer of the Ballet Ritz of New York.

"Look at her," one of the *corps de ballet* girls whispered while they waited backstage, stretching their calves and making sure their hairpins were secure, as Antoinette whirled and leaped in her great black cape. "The cape is doing most of the dancing!"

"But she's the prima ballerina! She's the most wonderful dancer in the world!" said another lovely and eager, but more kindhearted, dancer.

"She's a prima, but not for long," snapped her friend, and they all moved in a great wave of *glissades* out onto the stage, dressed as passengers at the railway station where Antoinette, as poor Anna, stood sadly thinking of all the losses in her life.

The jealous ballerina whispered, "She's so stuck-up,

I hope she gets her cape stuck under the fake train! Prima indeed!"

Just then, in the piano backstage, a momentous event was taking place. Mousie Child Six opened her eyes and said, "Prima! Of course! That is who I am. I will be the principal dancer of the Ballet Rodente."

"It's always good to set your sights high, but don't be too disappointed if you do not turn out to be the principal dancer," Mother cautioned her lovely little girl. "We must always be prepared to do our best, even if someone else is more accomplished. Our best is the best we can give."

"But *my* best is going to be the best ever. I was born to dance, Mother, and not just for mice," Prima explained. "I hope to dance for all the people in the world, for mouse people, human people, and even the occasional . . . creature."

"Oh, dear," Mother Pianissima told her sister Mezzanina later that night. "I'm afraid we've got a *real* prima on our hands here."

Mother Mezzanina then told Mother Snacketta, who was jogging down the stairs with her son

Sno-Cap because they both hoped to lose an ounce by summertime. "Well," Mother Snacketta puffed, "our sister Pianissima always *did* put on airs. Take yourself too seriously, and your children will do the same."

"Well," Mother Mezzanina replied, "so long as Prima stays in the piano, she'll be just fine."

But Prima had other plans. She already had her sharp black eyes on the big stage.

Mother Mezzanina, whose six children—Dusty, Fluff, Sneeze, Leg Room, Velvet, and Opera Glass— were all scholars and all perfectly well behaved, advised Mother Pianissima to take a firm hand.

Alas, sweet Mother Pianissima had a very tender heart. She found it very difficult to speak sharply to little Prima. Perhaps if she had, a great deal of hulla-baloo would have been avoided. But the world of mouse ballet might have missed out on a great deal of fun.

Who knows? Sometimes fun and a great big hulla-baloo can look very much like the same thing!

The Education of Miss Prima

ALL THE MOTHER mice first taught their daughters and sons the ordinary skills: flattening and jumping in emergencies, squeaking hysterically when cornered, bristling up their fur to look bigger when cats or humans were about. The father mice taught their sons and daughters trapping in the country style and built each of them a soda-bottle-cap Mousetrap Defeater, just their size, so they could survive no matter what circumstances life brought them. Father Pianissima left one Defeater in a trap for the kindly usher, Angelo, who didn't know what it was but kept it on his key ring anyhow.

But as the mouselets grew, Mother Pianissima and even Mother Snacketta undertook the instruction of their daughters and sons in the art of the dance. Occasionally even Madame Mousielle came down to watch and sat gravely in one corner, tapping her golden toothpick cane. Mother Pianissima demonstrated her star turn in *Giselle* as the doomed mouse maid. Even Father wept.

Once they had the children interested, they began with the positions—first, second, third, fourth, fifth position *en bas* and fifth position *en haut* (Madame would not *hear* of using the English translations "low" and "high"). They taught their children *grands battements* ("They're just large beats, bang, bang, bang," said jolly Pan) and *développés,* or extensions of the turned-out leg, at the old doorstop *barre* where their mothers had all learned their own steps. The *barre* had been hoisted down from the VIP box and set up backstage by the mouse fathers.

Quickly Mother Pianissima noticed that Prima's *développé* was much more developed than her other children's. Her leg was long and high and as steady as a young tree.

"*Superbe!*" whispered Madame. She began attending classes each night, her eyes on Prima.

And when it came to center-room work, Prima could crisscross her feet in the *entrechat* a full six times before landing, a feat beyond even the great Wayne Sleep, an acclaimed principal dancer, though unfortunately a human. He could do only five.

Then came the fateful day when little Prima asked to show her father a new step she had mastered all on her own.

Alas, it was the *pas de chat*!

"That does it!" Father grouched to Mother. "She's off to the country to live with my sister Milka and my parents! Did you see what she just did?"

Of course, polite mouse dancers don't do the *pas de chat*, for as you know, it literally means "the step of the cat," and for Prima, it meant trouble with a capital T! She got a tiny tap on her tiny rear from her papa's paw, and no after-dinner chocolate crumbs, a treat all the mouselets loved.

"There will be no cat dancing in my piano," Father told all the little mice. "There's enough trouble in this world!"

"But Daddy," Prima piped up, "it feels so good to jump like a cat!"

"Mother!" Father called. "Deal with your child!"

Mother Pianissima cuddled Prima and told her she understood how tempting it was to try all the steps. "My precious Prima, we are mice first and dancers second," she explained.

But Prima spoke up: "Not me," she said. "I am not a mouse who happens to be a dancer. I am a dancer who happens to be a mouse."

Onstage, at a Tender Age!

LESSONS WERE WONDERFUL fun, and Prima never minded practicing. Indeed, she danced all day, sometimes along the keys of the piano, accompanying herself with pieces such as *"Für Elise"* (Prima loved the "fur" part) and *"Clair de Lune,"* which reminded her that when the moon rose to its highest, after midnight, the theater belonged to mice.

At the age of two months, which made her almost a teenager in mouse years, Prima tried out for her first role. With her brothers and sisters, as well as mouse students from the Ballet Ritz and other studios in the

city, she auditioned for a part in *Whiskerella*. Naturally all the girl mouselets wanted the role of Whisk herself, the poor mouse girl transformed for one glorious night from a waif in sooty rags to a princess in crystal and lace.

Mother Pianissima was very nervous indeed.

She knew Prima had the purest talent of all the little mouse dancers, but she also knew that Prima tended to throw caution to the wind and try difficult things, even when she wasn't ready.

But after Madame and several other older ballet mistresses had put the mouselets through their paces, Prima was chosen for the title role—a great honor for a very young dancer.

Mother Pianissima worried about jealousy but had to admit that her smallest daughter's ability to learn complicated steps on the first try would make her shine in her debut with the American Ballet Rodente.

The production was set forth on a stage made from an overturned milk crate draped with golden tulle from the costume shop. In her farewell turn as a balle-rina, Mother Pianissima—who henceforth would devote her life to motherhood and the occasional dance instruction—took the roll of the Wicked Stepmouse. Mother was brilliant. But when Prima— her long lashes heavy with real tears, carrying in one paw the "glass slipper" she'd made from plastic wrap twirled around a safety pin—completed seven double *piqué* turns across the stage, a gasp rose from the society mice, who were seated on spools that had once held thread in a store that made men's suits. The watchers simply couldn't help compare their own children, many of whom were dancing in the show as well, with Prima.

After the ballet a few snobbish mouse mothers grumbled that *their* mouselets might be equally talented if they'd had as much special attention.

But one kindly mother set her canary-feather hat firmly on her head and spoke up.

"I'm sorry, but what you are saying is not true," she said. "I've known Maria Tailchief since we were mouselets together in lessons with Madame Mousielle. She was the best dancer I have ever seen, and even Maria didn't have as much talent in her whole body as her child has in the tip of her tiny tail."

The following month Prima performed in *The Sleeping Beauty.*

Father Pianissima was so excited, he invited some Trapper friends who had never been to the Ballet Jolie. He brought Mo Si Mu (who lived inside a beautiful old hatbox at the exclusive Chang's Suit Shop) and Toots and Scratch, two grimy-pawed mice who lived in the trunks of yellow taxis. Afterward they told Prima's proud papa that in their dreams that night, they were handsome princes.

In the all-city Mouselet Recital that spring, Prima further astounded by performing a world-record seven *entrechats* before landing in a *demi-plié.* "It's as if she is an angel with wings," old Madame Mousielle said. All the society mice were asqueak about the thrilling sight. Her growing reputation should have been enough attention for any little mouselet.

But something was afoot at the Ballet Jolie. Though she was not at all conceited about her gift, Prima *did* remember the words she had spoken as a baby—her vow to dance not just for other mice, but for all the world. And she decided that now was the time.

She yearned to dance when all the human ladies and gentlemen in diamonds and pearls, and especially the little girls in red velvet dresses, came to the Ballet Jolie.

And so, with her favorite brother, Pan, who liked a joke, she cooked up a plan. The Ballet Jolie was hosting a children's ballet, a new and sparkling version of *Peter Pan*. Using a piece of fishing wire they borrowed from their father's gear, the mouselets practiced lowering Prima down from the flies (the rafters of the theater) until she hung suspended in the middle of the stage, her arms in fifth position, low and arched as tender little tree limbs.

The next challenge was costuming.

"Well, we have hands, don't we?" Prima asked Pan. "The mice in *Cinderella* made a ball gown. All we have to make are wings. I'll get a tiny piece of sparkly ribbon from the costume shop, and I'll open the scissors, and when I say jump, you *assemblé* right down onto that handle as hard as you can, bro!"

Within a very short time, with only a few jumps

and a little spirit gum, they had made a pair of twin-kling pink wings.

"You know, Father is going to ground us for our whole *lives*," Pan said as the big night grew near.

"Plus, I'm going to *tell*," said Prokofiev, who wasn't much of a dancer but spent his time, after the theater closed, pretending he was conducting the theater's orchestra. He particularly liked tossing his head with his eyes closed and waving a straight pin.

"You just mind your own cheese wax, longhair!" Prima sassed.

Pavlova, who loved her sister dearly despite Prima's naughty ways, was gentler. "Little sister, couldn't you just be happy dancing with me and Swannie in *Swan Lake* at our next Rodente event?" Pavlova had a pet, a trained moth from the coatroom, who was to be allowed to flutter daintily, pretending to be a swan in flight during the production their grandmamma had planned for her grandchildren and a few other choice students.

"*I* do not dance with insects," Prima said proudly.

"Shush now!" Pavlova cried. "You've hurt Swannie's

feelings." Swannie made a small moth noise, which Pavlova translated. "She doesn't think she's a moth, you see. She thinks she's a swan."

"But *you're* a mouse," Prokofiev told his little sister, "and you're going to be a mouse living on crouton crumbs for a week if our dad finds out what you're going to do in the pirate scene."

"If you stop being such a big spoilsport, I'll give you my dessert," Prima promised.

"For two nights," Prokofiev insisted.

"Okay," Prima agreed.

"And only if it's chocolate, not sunflower seeds," her brother added.

"Enough already!" Prima shouted. "The least you could do is help!" And Prokofiev did help rig the harness for his sister.

Thus on the night of the performance, down came Prima, with Pan backstage spinning her round and round. She was dazzling, a rosy speck of light and motion, her ears wrapped in a miniature dancer's bow.

"Look!" cried all the little children in the audience, decked out for the occasion in their best red dresses and blue blazers. "It's the real Tinkerbell!" The little ballerina onstage who had practiced for months to dance the role of Tinkerbell was not at all pleased, however, and leaped gracefully across the stage to land an elbow on Prima's rear, sending her into the wings, flying for real, without her string. She landed on the great black felt hat of the teenager who was dancing the role of Captain Hook, and he jumped higher than he ever had in ballet class and yelled to his mother, who was standing backstage, "Yikes, Ma! I knew I should have stuck to baseball!"

Angry as any mouse with a sore paw, Prima jumped down from the pirate hat, rearranged her wings, and leaped up the many carpeted stairs to the light booth, where she positioned herself in front of the great pink spotlight.

Suddenly a great gasp rose from the crowd. An elegant little fairy, made huge by the light, was projected against the backdrop of London Town, performing her seven *entrechats* and, yes, a few *pas de chat* as well.

When the beautiful vision abruptly disappeared, Pan hightailed it for the concession stand. He knew

what was coming, and he didn't want to be home when it came. Sure enough, at that very moment Father Pianissima was dragging a very indignant young Prima into the piano by one ear and sitting her down.

"Please explain just what you think you were doing!" he demanded.

"Dancing, Papa, just as I was taught!" Prima said innocently, in her smallest mouse voice.

"We do not dance for human people!" Father shouted. "Ask your mother and your mother's mother! This could be the ruin of all of us."

Mother Pianissima, as proud as she was of her daughter's lovely movements, had to agree. She gave Prima a stern lecture. Didn't Prima realize how fortunate the mice of the Ballet Jolie were, with not only their art, but their comfortable home and their many relatives to play with? Didn't she realize that the humans who ran the theater could easily find a big fat cat to do the worst?

"Or a *rat* terrier," Father added. "Or even a ferret! I've seen it in my time, daughter. . . ."

"And we could lose our home and end up like the street mice we've all heard of—in the Dumpsters, out in the cold, or like the Delicatessas, always running from that awful one-eyed cat, Knockwurst," Mother warned.

"But that's so silly!" Prima cried, shocking all her brothers and sisters by daring to talk back. "The children see us and try to get us to jump into their coat pockets and give us treats and—"

"But children are not REGULAR humans!" Father silenced her. "HUMAN PEOPLE ARE AFRAID OF MOUSE PEOPLE. And the older they get, the more scared they get!"

"Oh, nonsense," Prima mumbled. "That's an old mouse tale."

"It certainly isn't!" Father said, shaking his finger at his daughter. "Mice may be smarter than humans, but humans run the world! Now, Prima, you are grounded in this piano for . . . a month! I'm going out for some peanut butter." And he slipped on his Defeater and left, hitting an F sharp on the way out.

"Be a good girl, Prima," Mother told her littlest girl. "I know you love to perform. It's in your family's blood. But why can't you wait until after the theater closes, the way your brothers and sisters do, and be happy in our American Ballet Rodente?"

"Humph!" Prima said, but she went off to bed, her wings drooping and a big pout on her face. She sat up all night making her toe shoes. Just as human ballerinas sew on their own ribbons, mouse dancers, when they are old enough to go *en pointe*, make their own toe shoes, usually of nutshells (from pistachio to peanut) coated with nail polish. These were peanut shells given to her by her cousin Sno-Cap Snacketta, and Prima packed the toes just right with foam from her nest and tied on ribbons to lace around her ankles with what was left of her beautiful pink wings.

Despite how angry Father was, Mother Pianissima could not help feeling proud when a friend from the Newsstand family told her that newspaper reviewers the next day had raved about the clever "special effects" in *Peter Pan*.

Enter Kristen, Stage Left

PRIMA WAS STILL grounded to the piano the following week when, with a stomp of high-heeled boots and a flourish of mink, the gorgeous Antoinette Brown—whose hair Prima noticed was the same color as her own shiny coat—returned to the Ballet Jolie. She was there to dance, and to choreograph, one of the most famous ballets: *Giselle.*

Frankly, the prima was not in a very good mood.

"What simpleton made this coffee?" she growled as the stagehands cowered. "It tastes like motor oil!"

"Why don't you drink some motor oil, then?"

a voice from somewhere whispered.

"Who said that?" Antoinette demanded. "Whoever said that, you're fired!"

But the coffee was not really the problem.

Though Antoinette was still a very fine dancer indeed, her days as a principal were numbered. She was getting older—not for a regular person, of course, but a dancer's life on the stage is short. Her pirouettes were no longer effortless triples but careful doubles. And on top of that, a younger and even more beautiful dancer was to perform poor, doomed Giselle, instead of Antoinette. She would dance the Wilis' queen.

Of course, to Prima's eyes, her mousy-haired namesake still was the most magnificent dancer in the world. And though Antoinette went banging around barking orders at everyone until all the dancers performing the spirits of heartbroken girls called Wilis had tears in their big, sad, painted eyes, Prima admired her spirit.

Father Mouse was almost as excited as he got right before *The Nutcracker*.

"Now, *this* is a ballet!" he told his children as they

munched their sprouts and cheese (while hunting that day, Father had found an entire half sandwich and, with the help of his brothers and children, had hauled it home, using a program as a sled). "You see, poor Giselle is a country girl, like my dear sister Milka. She thinks her lover, Loys, is a country lad, as I was. But it turns out he's truly a count or a duke or something, one of those highfalutin types! Her jealous boyfriend tells her the truth, and in her despair, she—"

"That's enough of that," Mother Pianissima reminded him. Most ballet stories tend to be very, very sad, and Mother didn't want the children to have daymares thinking about poor Giselle's fate.

One evening while Prima was idly plucking out "*Clair de Lune*" on the keys of the old grand piano, a little girl suddenly appeared in the wings. Prima scurried into the depths of her home and watched carefully as the little girl, who was wearing jeans and a sweatshirt that said "I Hate Ballet!" and whose mouse-brown hair was tangly as Prima's nest in the morning, plunked herself down on the piano stool, threw down her soccer backpack, and began playing with the keys. She sang some very naughty things, which she really didn't mean: "My mother's makeup looks just like a cat's! And plus, she's getting fat!"

"Well, who do you think you are?" a tiny voice inquired.

"I'm Kristen Kaya Lindsey Lisa Jessie Brown, for your information," said the little girl. "And I'm the daughter of the prima ballerina Antoinette Brown. And whom are youm?"

Prima was so thrilled, she almost jumped out onto the keyboard. But she remembered her father's words: *Human people are afraid of mouse people.* Still, she thought, this was a small human.

"I'm a fairy," she whispered.

"Oh, you are not," Kristen Kaya Lindsey Lisa Jessie Brown replied. "Fairies are made up. I'm almost ten, you know."

"I'm . . . a talking mouse!" Prima admitted then. "And I am a great dancer." (Kristen understood every word, as all children can understand most animal languages.)

"Tell me another one," Kristen said with a yawn,

and got out a package of Sno-Caps, which made Prima's mouth water. "You're probably a recording."

Prima quickly laced up her peanut shells and bounded onto the keys. The little girl jumped. Then she smiled a great, white smile with sparkling braces. Prima thought that the braces looked like gleaming rhinestones.

"You *are* a talking mouse!" she said in wonderment. "What's your name? Do mice have names?"

"Do mice have names! Yes, we have names. My name is Prima, in fact. I'm named after your mother!"

"My goodness," said Kristen. "How cute! But that's not really her name, you know. That's just what they call her. Among other things."

"And how come you have so many names?" Prima asked. "Do all human people have five names?"

"No. I'm named after my mother's five best friends. None of them was speaking to her when I was born, because she kind of has a temper, and she was raving around because she wouldn't be able to get in shape in time for *The Firebird* at the Toscana Ballet. She made it up to them by making them all my godmothers."

"Just like Flora, Fauna, and Meriwether!" Prima said, smiling.

"And Malificent!" Kristen laughed. "But isn't that the movie version, not the real ballet?"

"And for your information, *all* mice are talking mice," Prima went on. "Don't tell me you've never talked to a mouse in your *whole life*, and here you are almost ten years old! Why, I'm only four months old, and I'm already grown up!"

"I just never had the chance to talk to a mouse," Kristen told Prima. "I'd love a pet, but Mom says we travel too much, and dogs are messy, and fish are icky . . . she has an excuse for everything! Plus, even though I like *watching* the ballet and maybe I would even like to write a ballet, I hate taking ballet. I'm the worst one in my class!"

"Oh, you poor thing," Prima said sadly.

"But I'm a great goalie!" Kristen insisted. "I'm on the traveling squad! I love soccer!"

"What's a goalie? And how can you hate to dance?" Prima asked, spotting carefully and performing a little double pirouette.

Kristen shrugged. "Everyone's different." She sighed. "I love sports! I love books! But I can't play one note on the piano or sing at all! I wish my mother would get a clue! She thinks if you're not skinny and a ballet dancer, you practically don't exist. And boy, is she going to be hard to live with when she's not the top cat in the Ballet Ritz anymore."

"Cat?" Prima whispered, flustered, then realized it was a human expression. "So that's what they were talking about! All those girls in the *corps de ballet*, they're all jealous of her!"

"Well, she does drink a lot of chocolate macchiatos, and she thinks if it isn't a kind of food you chew, it won't make you fat." Kristen giggled. Prima, though she knew it wasn't very nice, giggled too. "But I'd love to have a regular mother, who didn't have to fly to Italy or England or France and drag me along all the time. And who didn't live on lettuce leaves. And plus I wish I had a brother or sister too; but my mom says I have to wait until she's forty or else she'll lose her waistline!"

"What does your dad think?" asked Prima.

"He says he'd love her if she weighed two hundred

pounds! But he owns a big computer company, and he's hardly ever around either. It's just Estrella, the housekeeper, and my toys and me. And my friends, whenever my mother lets them come over, which isn't very often at all."

She told Prima about the building where she lived. "It has its own swimming pool," Kristen said, and then added politely, "Can mice swim?"

"Excellently." Prima sniffed.

"Well, you'd like it then," Kristen said. "There's a really cute boy who's sixteen years old who comes to be the lifeguard when they have classes on Saturday morning. But he just calls me—"

"What?" Prima asked. "Princess, I'll bet?"

"No, goofy!" Kristen laughed. "He calls me 'funny face.' Because of all these *freckles*! Mostly I just go down there and swim by myself. I like to go way down by the blue tiles and pretend I'm a mermaid."

"A . . . mermaid?" Prima said uncertainly.

"Right!" Kristen went on. "Or I pretend I'm an otter."

"An otter?" Prima asked.

Kristen thought for a moment. "Kind of like a big, big mouse that lives in water. I pretend I'm an otter, with a little baby otter who's my baby sister."

"Right, no brothers and sisters," Prima said, her very small but very soft heart hurting for Kristen.

"And by the time I have one, I'll probably be in college!"

"What's college?" asked Prima.

"Why, college is where you go to learn how to write and speak like an adult . . . and, well, decide what you want to be when you grow up."

"Oh," Prima said quietly.

"What?" Kristen asked.

"Well, it's just that . . . mice don't know how to read and write," Prima admitted.

"So how would you sign your autograph when you do your performances?"

"With my paw print; as a matter of fact, I should have printed my paw on the program when I was in *Peter Pan*! Maybe I'll do that next time."

"You were in *Peter Pan*? I saw that!" Kristen exclaimed.

"I thought you didn't like ballet," Prima teased.

"I like to *watch* ballet! I even like the lights and the costumes. I'd like to paint the forests and castles and things—"

"You just don't like to do the dancing yourself."

"Exactly!" Kristen said. "And plus, my mom thinks it's ever so much better to be able to do a *pas de bourée* than score a goal from midfield! You know?"

"I guess I see . . . or I could if I knew what soccer was."

"I could take you to the park sometime and you could see me play!" Kristen said. "Estrella takes me on Saturday mornings. You . . . you could ride in my backpack!"

"That would be so fun. But Kristen, not like I want to bring up ballet all the time, but I was the giant mouse in front of the spotlight," Prima said modestly. "You know, the pink spotlight?"

"Wow! That was in all the newspapers! They thought it was fake, like a puppet!"

"Nope! Just little old me! I got in big trouble!"

"How neat is *that*!" Kristen said.

"Do you have your own room? That would be pretty neat too. Get this," Prima said, sitting down on the piano keyboard and dangling her toe shoes near Kristen's right hand. Kristen ever so slowly put out one finger and touched Prima's silky little head. "I have *five* brothers and sisters: Pan, Prokofiev, Prince Charmant, Pavlova, and Paris. *And* twelve cousins. And my mother is you-know-what, so pretty soon there'll be even more of us in the piano! How would you like that?"

"Very much, I think," Kristen said sadly.

"Don't worry," Prima told her. "You can touch my head. I don't smell bad or have rabies and I won't bite you. Human people might be afraid of mouse people, but mouse people aren't afraid of humans. We usually just like to stay out of your way."

"Well," Kristen said, ever so softly, "you don't have to stay out of *my* way. *Giselle* goes up just after *Mayerling* this year, so I'm going to have to spend a whole lot of time sitting around here during rehearsals, doing my homework while my mom yells at everybody. Maybe we could be . . . friends."

"I'd like that," Prima said, "but it has to be our secret. If my mother or father found out I was friends with a human, I'd be grounded for life!"

"Oh, I'm usually grounded too."

"Why?" asked Prima.

"Well, I don't think I'm doing anything wrong," Kristen said, "but I like dropping ice cubes out the window, and we live forty stories up, and then there was the time I got all the pizza places in our neighborhood to deliver pizzas to Markie Mandel, who lives the next floor down, twenty pizzas, all with ham and pineapple—"

"Now that would be fun!" Prima agreed. "I think I'd love pizza!"

"You've never had a pizza?" Kristen gasped. "Why, I'll bring you one tomorrow! Prima, I think you're my kind of . . . mouse!"

Lights! Places! Trouble!

TRUE TO HER word, Kristen brought pizza to the theater the next day. And the next. *And* the next. Prima fell in love with pizza—and with her new friend, Kristen—during the rehearsals for *Giselle*. As rehearsals were held during the day, because performances were held at night, the two girls got to spend many hours together after Kristen was finished with school in the early afternoon. Kristen also brought her laptop computer and began showing Prima the built-in dictionary, with its words and pictures. It didn't take too long for Prima to dip her paw in the dancers' eyeliner and trace the letters *m-o-u-s-e* on a sheet of paper. She couldn't wait to show off her new skill, but there was no one she dared show!

"This is delicious!" Prima cried over her first nibbles of a pepperoni slice with thick crust, even though she kept getting long strings of mozzarella on her paws. "May I save some for my brother Panda, I mean Pan? He loves food!"

"Sure," Kristen said. "And your mom and dad too."

"Eeeek!" Prima squeaked, "Remember, no talking about mouse-human chitchats! My parents would freak!" (She'd just learned this expression from Kristen.)

The girls talked about everything, including the wide world outside the Ballet Jolie, things which Prima could not even imagine. Buildings that had tops that nearly touched the clouds! Bagels dropped right on the sidewalk! Pets with coats! Other kinds of theater— opera and Broadway. Kristen brought her recordings, and the two listened to wonderful show tunes, such as the song "Till There Was You" from *The Music Man*. Soon Prima was learning the steps to a new kind of dance. She thought Kristen was a very pretty name. "Maybe one of my own little girls will want to be called that," she told Kristen. "My mother says it's time for me to think about when I'm going to get married."

"Married? At four months old?"

"Right. I'm just a kid at heart! But my dad wants me to marry Mo Si Mu's son from the suit shop, because those mouse kids get all the rice and vegetables they want. My dad's from the country, and he doesn't like us eating snack food all the time."

"Well, I like the song 'Till There Was You,'" Kristen said, changing the subject from marriage, which was the last thing on *her* mind. "My mother brought me up singing show tunes to me at bedtime whenever she was home, and so did our housekeeper, Estrella. This one is how I feel about you."

"Me too," Prima said. "I never dreamed I'd have a best friend who didn't have four feet."

When it was time for *Mayerling* to begin its run, the dancers in *Giselle* had to move to a new rehearsal space across the street, and Prima was heartbroken.

"Don't worry, Prima," Kristen comforted her. "I'll pop over here every day and visit."

Kristen didn't break her promise, and when

marvelous things began showing up in the old piano—rolls of ribbon, bags of toasted nuts, candle ends for chewing gum—Mother began to ask questions.

"Are you actually stealing things from the costume shop?" Mother Pianissima asked.

"Stealing?" sniffed Prima. "No! Anyhow, you and Grandmamma do!"

"Only on an as-needed basis," Mother said a little nervously. "And what's this thing?" she asked, holding up a long, thin, sparkling green object.

"A green pepper strip!" Prima said triumphantly. "See, I don't have to marry the mouse boy down the street to have fresh vegetables."

"Where did you get it, Prima?" Mother Pianissima asked.

"Ummm, maybe one of the dancers dropped it. You know, they never eat anything much, and it was probably her whole lunch, so she was probably starving by the end of the day."

"And what about all the greasy paw prints in your nest?"

"Uh, well . . ."

"Prima!" Mother said sternly.

"I got them from a human! So there!" Prima said. "But wait, Mother, she's a ballerina's daughter, so that's good, and she's ever so nice. In fact, she's the daughter of the prima—my namesake—Antoinette Brown, and she understands the mouse language, and she promised never to tell." Mother only shook her head, so Prima went for the gold. "And look at this, Mother!" Slowly, in the resin dust on the floor, she wrote *m-o-u-s-e*.

"What's that?" Mother asked.

"It's *human writing*! It says 'mouse'! And I can write 'Prima' and 'cat' and 'love' and all sorts of things! Kristen taught me!"

Mother Pianissima couldn't hide her awe. A mouse who could write! Perhaps the first paw-writing mouse on earth! And her own child! But she quickly became concerned about Kristen's familiarity with the Pianissimas' home. "I'm sure she's a nice child, and it is true she's just a child—humans do stay children ever so much longer than mouselets—but Prima—"

"And she wants to bring her friends Allie and Erika to see me dance, Mama! They're really nice too, and Kristen told them all about our family—"

"No, Prima! You can't be serious! You mean you allowed this little girl to tell her friends about us? Oh, goodness gracious," Mother said. "Dearest Prima, you've revealed us. Now humans will know that mice live in this piano! We'll be poisoned! I'm going to have to tell Father that we need to relocate. He'll be really sad. This has been our home for so very long!"

"Mother, please, please, don't," Prima pleaded. "Just as we're different from other mouse people, Kristen is different from other human people. She loves mice. And she is really good and kind. She would never, ever tell where we live. She understands the mouse language and everything!"

Mother Pianissima was deeply worried, but she decided to wait and watch before organizing an escape. And when she saw Kristen and Prima playing together, she knew that Kristen was indeed an extraordinarily gentle human being. "All right," she told Prima. "I understand why you like her so much. But please, Prima, don't do anything else to draw attention to us! If you do, I'll forbid you to see Kristen."

"But I want people to see me dance! If mice can watch human people dance, why can't human people watch mice dance? Wouldn't it make human people have more respect for us? It could change the whole tradition of mouse-human relations. It could get rid of traps, and I'd be a pioneer for peace." Prima complained, stomping her foot so hard her peanut-shell practice shoe broke.

"Enough! We know what's best," Mother said. "Plenty of mouse people will see you when you perform with the Ballet Rodente."

"Oh, shipoopi!" Prima cried.

"I'll have no swearing in my piano!" Father said, coming in with an armload of peanut-butter crackers and removing his helmet.

"Oh, Dad, it's only a word from a song that Kristen played—"

"Kristen. Who's Kristen?" Father asked sharply.

"One of Prima's friends, from down the way," Mother explained hurriedly, not quite telling a fib. Prima glanced at her mother and smiled.

"A Newsstand Mouse child," Mother continued.

*   *   *

As Christmas approached, Prima introduced her brothers and sisters, one by one, to Kristen. Then she told Kristen about the surprise she and her siblings were planning for their father, during opening night of *The Nutcracker*, in one month's time.

"We are going to challenge the Mouse King!" Prima whispered.

"How?" Kristen asked.

"Well, we're going to make ourselves into one giant *m-o-u-s-e*!" Prima explained. "We're making Defeaters—those are the helmets my father invented—for all of us. Two of us are going to stand on Pan's shoulders, and the other four are going to stand behind and in front, and we're going to charge down the aisle. Our dad is going to be so proud, and so are all our uncles! You know, I should get my cousins in on this."

"Then you could be an *m-o-u-s-e* with eighteen heads!" Kristen cried. "Hey! I could let you use my doll wagon—"

"Yeah!" Prima agreed. "Then we could all get a big push and ride down—"

"Yep," Kristen said with satisfaction. "It's going to be great, but you'll sure get in trouble."

"That's what I'm worried about," said gentle Pavlova.

"No, Father loves a good battle," Pan told Pavlova. "He'll like it. Mother will too."

Was Pan ever mistaken!

Here is how Prima's greatest disaster (or her greatest achievement, depending on how you look at it) began.

Armed with their Defeater helmets and the plastic cocktail swords their cousin Chewy Snacketta had given them, the six little Pianissimas hid themselves in the branches of the great Christmas tree that rises from under the stage during the well-known ballet. Prima had never been more excited as she peeked from behind the red velvet curtains and saw the patrons take their seats.

"It's a full house!" she cheered. Pavlova and the rest picked up their cocktail swords. As they watched Clara fall asleep with her toy nutcracker clutched in her arms, they were thrilled that their moment of glory was almost upon them.

"Places!" Prima finally cried, and the five other little Pianissimas chorused, "Ready, set, go!"

Just as the battle with the Mouse King began, the six Pianissima children leaped in true Pianissima form from tree branches and attacked.

On the stage, pandemonium reigned. Clara jumped up on the bed, and Herr Drosselmeyer tried to slip beneath the sofa. The Mouse King, peering through his masked head, finally spotted the source of all the running and screeching: six little mice with swords! He fled from the stage, losing two of his heads in the process.

In fact, Father Mouse *was* proud, but he knew such hijinks were dangerous. Mother Pianissima grounded all six little mice for the rest of the run and made them spend each night springing traps for the whole family.

"Nyah, nyah," chubby cousin Gumdrop Snacketta teased. "Caught again."

"A cowardly mouse dies a thousand deaths but a brave mouse dies but one!" Prince Charmant retorted, defending his sister. But everyone knew something had to be done.

Mother Pianissima told her sister Mother

Mezzanina, "I don't know what to do about Prima. She's already rehearsing for *Romeo and Juliet*!" Mother Mezzanina suggested using some of that new ribbon to tie up Prima on show nights.

But Mother Pianissima was too sweet to do such a thing.

And sure enough, during the balcony scene, critics noticed that the ballerina who played Juliet kept watching her feet as though she was trying not to step on something, though her *entrechats* showed astounding height and she seemed to be improvising new leaps.

That night Father laid down the law. He personally was going to find a furniture van and take Prima to New Jersey to live on the farm. "This child is completely out of paw," he said, "and that is that."

"It wasn't just Prima," Mother reminded him.

"It was her idea!" Father roared.

"Well," said Mother, "she does get that from you."

"True," Father said with a sigh. And by the next morning, though he still brought up the farm, he was a little less angry and a little more proud.

The Great Escape

PRIMA WAS SADLY *soutenu*-ing the tune "*Clair de Lune*" on the keyboard when Kristen arrived the next day. With a few tears and a great many gulps, Prima poured out the whole story.

"Poor baby Prima!" said Kristen when she heard about her friend's impending banishment from the Ballet Jolie. "There's got to be a way out of this," she added. Twisting a strand of her curly hair, she became lost in thought.

"I don't see how." Prima pouted. "Mice have to obey their parents. It's simply rodental tradition. And my dad said that as soon as the farm cousins come for *The Nutcracker*, Aunt Milka is taking me back with her."

"How do the mice on the farm know about you getting into trouble?"

"Dad sent word through the mouse chain," Prima explained.

"What's that?" Kristen asked.

"Well, one mouse tells another mouse, who tells another mouse who lives a little farther away, and pretty soon the word's out all over the place! I'll end up married to a country pumpkin!"

"I think you mean bumpkin," Kristen said with a smile.

"Same difference," Prima said, sitting down on middle C with a sigh.

"Give me one night to think this over," Kristen said. "And don't give up hope! Tomorrow is the premiere of *Giselle*, and my mom is going to be so distracted—"

"What's your *mom* got to do with it?" Prima asked.

"Don't you worry your pretty pink ears," Kristen

said. "Mice aren't the only ones who can come up with schemes!" Kristen's gray eyes seemed to sparkle with excitement. Prima knew her friend was hatching a plot. She couldn't wait to hear what it was.

Prima waited impatiently the next night, and Kristen finally showed up. She'd slipped away from her father and the other guests in tuxedos and beaded gowns, all society humans who were excited to see the new version of the ballet. For a moment Prima hardly recognized Kristen. She was wearing her hair braided up in ribbons, and a rose-colored lace dress with patent-leather shoes. And she was carrying an extremely large patchwork purse of many colors.

"Okay, Prima, the time has come to sit or jump off the piano," Kristen told Prima, while Prima's mouse brothers and sisters listened from behind the keyboard. "My plan is this: When the ballet is over, you'll jump right into this bag, and I'll carry you home."

"Home?" Prima cried. "I *am* home!"

"I mean home to my house, my penthouse!"

Pan and Pavlova wailed together, "Sister, no!"

"It's better than the farm," Prima said soothingly. "Let Kristen explain."

"Well, I live in a big, big apartment, high up on top of one of the biggest buildings in New York. Why, we even have trees in pots right outside our door on a big terrace. You could live in my room and sleep with me in my castle bed, or in one of my doll beds. I have a real puppet theater we could make into a mouse dance theater. It would be much nicer than the American Ballet Rodente—oh, I don't mean that the Ballet Rodente isn't nice—but this has real velvet curtains and a wooden floor and it's just the size for a mouse, and we could have ballets for you to star in, in the middle of the night, and I could paint the sets with my paint set! And I'd bring you food every day . . . what do mice eat?"

"Anything!" Pan cried.

"Mostly chocolate," Prima said primly. Then she panicked. "But what about your mother? And what about ours?" Prima wasn't at all sure Mother

Pianissima would allow her daughter to go out alone into the world, and suddenly the old piano seemed like a very safe place.

"Well, I know your mother would *much* rather have the chance to see you perform and maybe even visit you at my house than have you go all the way to New Jersey to live!" Kristen declared. "And Pavlova and Prokofiev and the rest could come for sleepovers! I've always wanted a pet—not that you're a *pet*, exactly, Prima, because you're my best friend, but my mother won't let me have one—"

"This could actually work!" Prima said. She scurried into the piano to talk to her mother and father. Mother and Father Pianissima were surprised, but not entirely unhappy. They knew that the old piano was too small to contain a talent and an adventurous heart as big as Prima's. "You know, Mama, I don't want to go to New Jersey. I'm a city mouse. And I'm grown up now and have to make my own decisions. And I've always wanted to go on the road, Papa. I guess I get my yearning for taking risks from you!

Kristen says they live on Fifth Avenue, right near some cousins of the Delicatessas, so I could always send a message through the chain if I needed to, and I'll come back and visit."

"It does sound exciting." Mother sighed, musing on her days as a dancer.

"And it would allow her to see the world, Mother," Father added a little reluctantly. He hadn't really wanted to send Prima back to the farm, but he had not been able to see another way to end her mischief. Still, now that the time for leaving had actually arrived, he realized how much he would miss his smallest, most rascally daughter.

"She'll even go flying on planes," Kristen added softly, because the *corps de ballet* girls were entering the wings, each one fondly patting Kristen on the head for luck. "She could go to France! And Italy!"

"Magnifique!" Mother whispered, remembering her mother's stories of her homeland. "Father, how can we deny her that?" Backstage the human dancers were getting into position for their entrances, and Kristen's

mother arrived in a tizzy. This abruptly ended the conversation, and all the Pianissimas rushed back into the deepest reaches of the piano.

"Straighten your back, Chelsea!" she whispered angrily. "Anna, the ribbon in your hair is hanging down like a mouse tail!"

"Wait a minute there!" Prima began to squeak angrily.

"What is that awful screech?" Antoinette Brown asked.

"A . . . a violin string broke, I think, Mom," Kristen said. The overture began, and the dancers tiptoed delicately onto the stage. "Prima, hush now. You will mess up the plan!"

"Kristen Kaya Lindsey Lisa Jessie Brown, get to your seat this instant!" Antoinette Brown told her daughter. "The performance has begun!"

"I have to go now, but I'll be back after the show, and Mother and Father Pianissima, I promise, I'll take awfully good care of her!" Kristen whispered. "I love her so!"

If they knew one thing, the Pianissimas knew that this was true.

And finally, finally, after a talk that took up half the first act, they gave Prima their permission.

So while *Giselle* was being performed, mice were racing all over the theater, helping Prima collect peanut shells for extra toe shoes (they didn't know if suitable peanut shells for toe shoes existed outside the Ballet Jolie), and Father was quickly constructing a new Defeater helmet for his girl, and the aunties, uncles, and cousins were coming to kiss Prima good-bye.

As soon as the final curtain call was over, Kristen was out of her seat and looking for her mother. The show had been a rousing success; surely by now her mother had recovered from her hissy fit and was feeling pretty pleased with herself.

Kristen found her in the lobby, dropping peach roses from her bouquet and signing autographs for people who begged to touch her hand. Kristen asked, "Mommy! Is it okay if I bring a dancing mouse home with us?"

Antoinette, who thought her little girl was pretending again, airily answered, "A dancing mouse? Yes, of course, darling! Now get your coat; we've got to run home for the reception!"

Kristen rushed backstage to the piano with the good news. She could see from the mixed emotions on the faces of the Pianissimas (mice *do* have many expressions; it's just that they're usually moving so quickly, humans can't quite see them—and they often don't want to!) that Prima's parents had said yes as well.

"It's honestly the best thing for Prima!" Mother Pianissima said to Kristen as they were loading Prima's belongings into Kristen's purse. "I can't really see her learning to hang from udders and milk Patience the cow the way her Aunt Milka used to do when she was young. But I will miss her so much!"

"And so will we!" cried Pavlova, Paris, Pan, Prokofiev, and Prince Charmant. Even the moth, Swannie, made a tiny noise that sounded like "awk!" Pavlova said it meant that Swannie would miss Prima too.

Finally it was time for Kristen and Prima to leave.

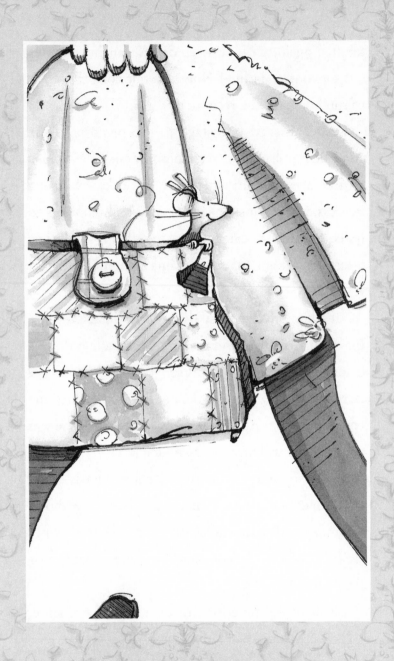

Pretending to be too gruff to hide his real sorrow, Father Pianissima hugged his little girl and told her to remember she was a Trapper's daughter at heart. "Be sure you get enough to eat," he told her kindly. "No one likes a scrawny mouse. Look at your mother, plump as a—"

"That will do," Mother said, then added, "I suppose with a talent like yours, we couldn't expect to keep you cooped up in the old piano forever." But there was a tear in her eye as she kissed her daughter good-bye.

Then, with her tiny heart pounding, Prima jumped out of the piano and into Kristen's patchwork purse.

Prima on the Town

PRIMA'S FIRST EXPERIENCE in the world outside the Ballet Jolie was a short ride in a long, white limousine filled with fancy humans all clinking tall glasses and telling Antoinette Brown that she was truly a genius—something Antoinette smiled at and didn't bother to deny.

All Prima could do was listen and peek out through tiny holes in the fabric of Kristen's purse, but she was wild with excitement.

"Is this a fairy coach?" she asked Kristen.

"Kind of," Kristen explained. (She wasn't really

worried about talking to Prima in the crowded limo, as none of Antoinette's friends ever bothered to listen to her. But just in case, she sang the words so that if anybody heard, they would assume she was singing to herself.)

"Then where are the horses and coach mice?"

"Well, it runs with an engine . . . oh, gee, you don't know what an engine is. It's kind of like pretend horses, only they're electric. It's called a car."

"Oh, I've heard of *cars!*" Prima sniffed. "They're monsters that run over you-know-whats. *C-a-t-s*." She spelled the dreaded word correctly.

"Uh, right," Kristen said, smiling brightly at everyone and pretending she was singing "Till There Was You" but hoping no one would notice the words. "Now, shush, Prima. We're almost home."

Soon they were in a lush and beautiful penthouse high above the city. Prima caught a glimpse of a huge living room with two grand pianos, one black and one white. Later on she would discover that the apartment had five bedrooms, each a different color and each color like a lovely piece of ripe fruit, and a library with more books than Prima would be able to chew on in her entire lifetime!

Finally they were safe in Kristen's room, after a quick trip through the living room to snag a few chocolate-covered strawberries and some lemon tarts from the buffet table. They could hear the reception guests milling through the rest of the penthouse, but it seemed far away as Prima popped her head out of the beautiful velvet patchwork purse and took her first look at her new home. She couldn't believe her eyes! Kristen lowered her friend gently to the carpet—plush as the pile of velvet in the costume shop—so that she could explore the room, which Kristen's father had built for his daughter as a special haven.

Kristen was a friendly girl, but since her mother was always deciding that no school was good enough, she'd changed schools six times since kindergarten. Her grades were good, but it didn't matter. She always got admitted because *everyone* wanted the famous Antoinette Brown's daughter at their private school. But it didn't make it easy for Kristen to get close to people her own age.

She did have a few true friends, but one lived far away in Westchester and one across town on the other side of Central Park, which sometimes seemed just as far. They talked on the telephone and Kristen had friends over once a month, but that wasn't the same as playing together every day.

Not that she would have had time with all the ballet and music lessons, ones that Kristen didn't want, and all the practice for sports, which she did want, and all the books she so loved to lose herself in.

Being Kristen was not easy. It wasn't like being every other little girl. But just as Prima's papa understood her, so did Kristen's father, George, understand *her*.

Kristen's dad had wanted to be an architect, but his own father made him run a big computer company instead. He knew a lot about the pressures of living up to other people's expectations and realized that his little girl might need to escape from the endless parties, travel, and publicity a celebrity's daughter had to endure. So he had made her a bedroom that was a child's paradise.

The bed was a castle high in the air. It was painted

as if it was made of gray bricks. Kristen climbed up into it using a ladder her father had painted to look like a castle's drawbridge. She had silky curtains she could draw around her bed, and the bed was round, with room enough for three friends, for those times when Kristen had sleepovers. The ceiling lights were the shape and soft milky color of stars.

Beneath the bed was a desk for doing homework, but the desk chair was a throne covered in purple velvet.

Kristen even had her own refrigerator, where she kept juice, yogurts, jars of paint, and sometimes broken birds' eggs and other funny things. In the corner across from the bed hung a golden fishing net for all of Kristen's sports equipment, and next to this was a low table holding a beautiful antique puppet theater. After exploring the theater, Prima decided that it had really been built to order for mice. There was even a tiny trapdoor for special effects. Prima dreamed of staging her own version of the *The Nutcracker* for Kristen and her friends, and perhaps even her idol, Antoinette!

But when she spoke of her plans, Kristen warned her, "I think we'd better keep you a secret, at least for now." She petted Prima's soft, downcast head with one finger and went on, "You know that human grown-ups won't understand you are a great artist as I do, Prima dear. They will see only a mouse. So when I am at school, I think it's best you stay right in here. Our housekeeper, Estrella, will chase you with a broom and smack you if she can. I'll leave you plenty of food and milk when I'm gone."

As it transpired, Prima wasn't even tempted to explore the rest of the apartment.

Kristen's room was a mouse paradise, and ever so much better than the dear piano at the Ballet Jolie. It was bright and colorful and filled with places to hide whenever Estrella came in, humming happily, to clean and put fresh sheets on Kristen's bed.

As soon as Estrella closed the door, Prima would jump up onto the radiator and then onto the window seat. She never got tired of looking out, and if Kristen left the window cracked, she would slip outside onto the ledge. From there, she could look right down on

Central Park, on the beautiful rocks and trees and pools of water. For the first time, Prima could see the human world from above. Mother had *never* allowed the mouselets to climb out onto the roof of the Ballet Jolie. She saw trees, grown humans with baby humans in chairs on wheels, and huge animals (horses?) that pulled human people in real princess coaches. She saw giant cats that made *Woof! Woof!* noises pulling humans along on long strings of leather and realized that being pulled on leather strings must be another way that humans got from place to place.

She waved to all the birds, and to society mice who flew by on pigeon taxis. Once a pigeon taxi stopped, and Prima sent a paws-card to her mother on Kristen's purple paper. The elderly passenger was a friend of Madame Mousielle's, and more than happy to do the favor.

At night, after Kristen's soccer games and dance lessons, Prima practiced her exercises at a *barre* Kristen made for her from Popsicle sticks, while Kristen did her homework. Kristen taught Prima to type by dancing on the computer keyboard, just as she had played music by dancing on the keys of the Pianissima home. Pretty soon, she could play computer games with Kristen and, being a mouse, was even faster with her feet than Kristen was with her fingers. Her favorite game was, of course, Mousetrap. Within just a few weeks, she was able to type out a letter. The next time she saw the kindly grandmouse pass by on a pigeon taxi, she waved and asked if the grandmouse would walk *very slowly* up to Angelo, the kindly usher at the Ballet Jolie, and hand him the letter, which was folded to the size of a human postage stamp.

The front of the letter read, "Please read this letter out loud while standing in front of the broken piano backstage left. Thank you very kindly." Angelo nearly jumped a foot when he was handed a tiny piece of paper by a silver-backed mouse, but he wasn't really very frightened, and he did as the letter asked. So Mother Pianissima, to her great surprise, was able to hear that though Prima missed her family more than all the peanut butter in paradise, her daughter was being good, practicing every day, sleeping in a tiny bed with a silk pillow, learning all sorts of new things, and eating twelve meals a day as every mouse should. Mother was also excited to hear that soon, when Antoinette and George were out of town, Prima and Kristen would come in a car one night and bring the whole family to see Prima's new home. Prima was practicing the principal's solo from *The Firebird* on Kristen's stage to show her family.

Some nights, when Antoinette was dining out late, Kristen turned on the talking box in which tiny human people performed all kinds of shows all day and night. But best of all, Prima and Kristen liked to look out the window. For Kristen, it was as though she was seeing the world through brand-new eyes. She explained to Prima that the cars with the big flashing lights and whooping sirens carried police officers rushing to help humans in trouble; that the yellow cars that honked all night long were taxis. Taxi drivers just honked, Kristen said, because it was part of their job.

They also occasionally threw ice cubes down to make humans jump and look up to see why ice was falling from the clear, dark blue night sky. And Prima saw another mouse in the window directly across from her window. That mouse told other mice in his building, and soon mice of all ages were waving to Prima from ten windows next door.

"Wow," Prima said to Kristen one night, "I wish all those society mice who used to come to see our ballet could see me now!"

"What are society mice?"

"Well, they're mice who have houses like this, behind the walls of . . . well, apartments like yours, Kristen. They very slowly borrow little bits of cotton and make beds, and little bits of ribbon to make curtains, and they take the mirrors when human ladies throw away their makeup holders."

"Where do they live?" Kristen asked.

"Grandmamma used to say she had friends who lived in Trump Towers and the Palladino," Prima said proudly.

"Prima, this *is* the Palladino!" Kristen told Prima.

"Take my hand, Kristen," Prima said, holding out one paw. "I'm a stranger in paradise."

Debut and Danger!

IT WASN'T LONG indeed before Father and her elder siblings came to see Prima's "palace," as they called it, and to watch her short piece from *The Firebird*. Only Mother and gentle Pavlova stayed home to mind the new litter of mouselets. Before calling the car service and helping everyone gently into her backpack for the ride to her home, Kristen promised Mother that she would bring Prima to see her new baby brothers and sisters, as well as to attend the wedding of Paris, who was marrying the son of Father's old friend Mo Si Mu from the suit shop in just a few weeks.

Father kissed Prima good-bye and told her how sorry Mother was that she wouldn't be able to attend Prima's most ambitious performance at what Prima now called the Ballet Palladino, since she was still nursing the new mouselets. "We're very, very proud of you, Prima," he said.

"Why, in your own way, you've come as far as your grandmother did! You're a mouse *voyageuse!*" Father boomed in as full-throated a boom as a mouse can make.

Prima modestly peered down at her peanut-shell shoes, which Kristen had painted red and black for the performance. She was a well-bred mouse and knew better than to act stuck-up in front of her very own family. But she was quietly very satisfied.

On the night of the big performance of *The Girl Who Needed Watching*, starring Prima Pianissima as Lise, Prima got out of the doll bed where she sometimes slept (when she wasn't sleeping on Kristen's own pillow) and immediately began to practice. She and Kristen had drawn cardboard puppets Kristen could move from beneath the stage to represent the male dancers, Alain and Colas, as well as Lise's poor, confused mother—who, just like Prima's own mother, doesn't know what to do with her high-spirited daughter.

The society mice came reluctantly. All Prima had to do was call out to her acquaintances one building over and the word was out. Still, even though word of mouse around Fifth Avenue had it that Kristen was one of those rare human beings (those called, among rodents, "trusted ones," like the scientist Marie Curie and the writer E. B. White) who wouldn't put out cookies laced with heaven *knows* what, they weren't all that keen to go to a strange penthouse. It was well known that child humans were better than the other kind, but you never knew. Boy humans had been known to do unspeakable things.

They did come, however, because rumor had it that Madame Mousielle, who never left the Ballet Jolie, might be present. Other mice came too. Some of them were white mice who were pets (who could, of course, get out of their cages anytime they chose). They knew more about humans and were bolder. But Prima's audience refused to pay even one peanut—sure that a little mouse who wasn't from the Upper East Side would be no match for the talents of their own sons and daughters. Prima wasn't at all concerned. "Confidence comes from within," she told Kristen.

Kristen blinked her light switch twice in the room to announce the beginning of the performance, and Prima reached down to retie one of her peanut-shell shoes.

Just then there came an odd tapping at the window. It was so loud, Kristen was afraid that her mother, who was having a few friends over for dinner, might hear the noise, so she went to investigate. And there, on the windowsill, rap-tapping with her golden toothpick, was Madame Mousielle herself!

"Grandmamma!" Prima cried. "How did you ever manage to get here?"

"I hailed a pigeon," Madame explained. "It's not

that difficult. But it's the first time I'd taken one in years, and the price has gone up, *chérie!* One could fly all over New York for a single peanut or a piece of popcorn in my youth! Now it's two peanuts for a short hop! And it's made me rather dizzy."

Of course, the society mice were simply awed by having the great ballet mistress in their midst.

"Prima," Madame explained, "is my grand-daughter. Though I do not wish to seem vain, I believe she is the finest pupil I have ever taught. I hope you will agree." Madame placed her hand on the windowsill and swayed a bit. "I think I feel faint!"

Kristen ran out into the solarium, into the midst of her mother's party. She cried, "Help! I need a thimble and a . . . I need a thimble and a pincushion!" Everyone stared. "It's for a school project," Kristen stammered to the crowd of thin, silent guests, with their elegantly painted eyes and long, silky, black dresses and double-breasted suits. "It's an emergency!"

Estrella, who sometimes worked party evenings (and always stayed with Kristen overnight when her parents were away), had been serving shrimp on toast

from a silver tray. She quietly went to the broom closet and brought back the sewing basket. Kristen took it and ran from the room.

"Kids! Aren't they something?" Antoinette Brown remarked lightly to her bemused guests.

Back in her bedroom, Kristen locked the door and sat Madame Mousielle down on the pincushion and gave her a thimbleful of cold water. When the elderly mouse was calm, the ballet began.

Prima had never been so luminous. She leaped with the grace of a butterfly; she landed with the lightness of a feather. The society mice wept when it seemed that Lise would lose her beloved, and cheered when it was revealed that Colas was indeed Alain, the son of a rich aristocrat, whose father loved Lise's mother's delicious cooking. Afterward, over a chocolate crêpe Kristen nicked from her mother's cocktail party and divided into small portions, they admitted that Madame's granddaughter was indeed a treasure of ballet.

When Kristen announced that the next ballet, *Coppélia*, which one of Prima's sisters would also dance, would be held at the Ballet Jolie so that dozens of mice could attend, the society mice were quick to sign up for the show.

As they shouted, "Brava! Brava!" Prima had a strange feeling. She was so happy that, instead of laughing, a tear rolled down her cheek. Truly Prima did not know whether she was happy or sad. She missed her mother very much and hugged her grandmother tight before the old mouse flew off into the moonlight on the back of another pigeon.

As Prima climbed into bed that night, she remembered what her mother had told her—that shedding tears for the combination of happiness and sadness simply meant a mouse was growing up. But Prima wasn't *ready* to grow up. She worried about this most of the night, until she fell asleep in the morning, wondering what it would be like to grow up, to fall in love, to have a litter. It seemed as though such things might be a little boring and take up all a mouse's time too— but also be entrancing in a strange sort of way.

But in the morning, something happened that wiped all these dreamy thoughts from her mind like a wet eraser wipes writing from a chalkboard.

Antoinette, who, despite her willful ways, really did love her little girl very much, had become worried about reports from Estrella. The housekeeper idly mentioned that she often heard Kristen in her room alone, talking to herself in different voices, and she was sure that Kristen was removing the peanut butter from the mousetraps Estrella set each month.

So early in the morning, Antoinette tiptoed into Kristen's room, brushed the stuffed toy mouse off her daughter's pillow, and said, "Happy early birthday, darling heart. I've a surprise for you." And from behind her back, she pulled a tiny puffball, a blue-eyed Siamese kitten. "Here's a special friend for you, so you won't be so lonely. This is Meowsky."

A Whole New World

WHILE KRISTEN GOT ready for school, Prima spent an unhappy hour high atop the window frame while Meowsky curled up cheerfully in Prima's very own satin doll bed.

"What can I do, dearest Prima?" Kristen asked, reaching up from the window seat to stroke her friend. "If I say I don't want him, they'll think I'm nuts and send me to a psychiatrist! I've been begging for a kitten since I learned how to say the word!"

"I can always go back to my piano!" Prima said proudly, drawing herself up to her full two inches and nearly losing her balance in the process.

"Now, you don't want to do that," Kristen crooned in a voice that sounded to Prima suspiciously like a purr. "I'll think of something. Stay out of . . . harm's way, okay? You're a big girl, and you can take care of yourself. I'll leave the window open just in case you need to . . . well, make a quick exit to the fire escape. And let me think this over at school. Now I have to run or I'll be late!"

As soon as Kristen left, Meowsky smiled a lazy cat smile and, slowly, slowly unsheathed his tiny, pearly claws. At that moment Prima, ballerina though she was, actually did lose her balance. She fell directly where Antoinette had swept her earlier that morning, onto a pile of Kristen's jeans and T-shirts. Maybe, she thought in terror, cats really were dumb, like the giant woofing pullers she saw down in the street. She decided to pretend to be a stuffed toy mouse, just as Kristen's mother had thought.

"No use," Meowsky said in a sweet, slurring voice that made Prima's ears tremble. "I mighta been born at night, but it wasn't last night! I know you're fakin' it. I heard you talking to the girl!" Meowsky picked his way delicately over the pile of jeans and T-shirts on which Prima lay. "Hey there, tippy-toes," he purred. "I *know* you're fakin' it. I might look like a society cat, but I come from Brooklyn. Out there, mice like you are a dime a dozen."

"I beg to differ," Prima said, jumping up. "I happen to be a ballerina, an artist mouse of the first order!"

"What you look like to me is—you should pardon the expression—the feline equivalent of milk and cookies."

"If you try to eat me, I'll scream," Prima threatened.

"And who'll listen to ya?" Meowsky went on softly, examining his claws. "If old Estrella out there sees me with a mouse, I'll just get extra chicken bits in my kibble tonight. The way I see it, I'm in and you're history."

Prima, remembering she was a Trapper's daughter at heart, searched her mind for a quick comeback. "Well, you could commit murder, but it would be on your soul forever. And you'd break Kristen's heart. Want to spend your life with a little girl who hates the sight of you?"

"Cats don't much care about that sort of thing." Meowsky shrugged. But Prima could tell he was troubled. He really was only a kitten, away from home for the first time and trying to talk bigger than he actually felt. A little of Meowsky's swagger seemed to shrink. He licked his paws sadly.

"You know, I was born in the Ballet Jolie, and I was just thinking last night how much I miss my mother and my brothers and sisters, plus my grandmamma is so old, I'll probably never see her again," Prima said. Meowsky's big blue eyes blinked and seemed to fill with soft mist.

"Yeah," he said. "There was only two of us. Me and my sister, Kitt. She howled opera, Kitt. And Mom. Wonder what they're doing now."

"So what I figure is we should make the best of it," Prima said. "We have to share this place, and we have to share Kristen, for a long time—"

"Whoa, whoa, there, mousie-puss," Meowsky said. "Not such a long time, if you think it over. What I got in front of me is sixteen, seventeen years if I'm lucky. What you got is . . . maybe two, and from the looks of you, one of them is almost gone."

Prima gulped. "You mean mice live only two years?"

Meowsky replied, "Well, no one ever accused rodent types of being too smart. Carnivores: that's where the brains are in the animal kingdom, no offense intended. But did you ever notice that you could learn things in one day that would take Kristen months and months of work?"

"Ummm, yes," Prima replied, thinking of her *entrechats* and her computer skills.

"Well, that, Miss Mouse, is because you ain't got a whole lot of time to learn 'em," Meowsky said. "I don't mind sharing the joint with you. You scratch my back and . . . I won't scratch yours. But I'm the boss, get it? I'm the predator. Sorry to stomp your day."

Prima went and lay down on her bed. She stared at the ceiling and, for the second time in two days, she began to cry.

She thought hard about things her mother had told her. Mother Pianissima often said "tomorrow" or "next week," but come to think of it, she never said, "next year." In fact, Prima didn't really know what a "year" was. She knew that Grandmamma was old; and she knew that meant she wouldn't always be with them, but she didn't exactly know what that meant. That just wasn't the way mice thought about time—or life, for that matter. *Were* meat eaters really more clever? On the other paw, she thought, Meowsky would soon be a big, fat *c-a-t*. Maybe he was lying.

When Kristen came home, Prima got up and asked whether what Meowsky had told her was true.

Kristen's sweet gray eyes filled with tears, and then the tears spilled over, but she tried to be brave for Prima. After all, Kristen had learned about the life span of mice from her teacher only two days before.

"Yes, Prima," she said. "It is true. But the good thing is this. It doesn't *feel* like only two years, for you. Think about it. A human person would still be a baby after nine months. And you're a *teenager*! So you'll have a long, full life, and an exciting one. For one thing, guess what? After *Coppélia* is over at the Ballet Jolie, we're going to Europe!"

"*In an airplane?*" Prima gasped.

"Yes, in first class," Kristen said.

"Me too," Meowsky purred.

"Only if you're good," Kristen said.

"You missed part of what he said, Kristen," Prima added quickly. "He said he's afraid of flying"—she noticed that Meowsky suddenly flexed his sharp little claws—"but that he can overcome it."

"Well, as I said, he can come if you two can be friends," Kristen said, giving Meowsky a stern look. Kristen really did think Meowsky was a beautiful kitten, with eyes as bright as crystal beads. But Prima stuck out her tongue at Meowsky, as if to whisper *See there?*

When Kristen's real birthday arrived, she asked her mother for a special present.

"What I'd really like, Mommy, is a sewing machine," Kristen said.

"A *sewing* machine?" Antoinette Brown asked in shock. "Whatever for?"

"To make . . . doll clothes," Kristen replied sweetly.

Her mother's eyes widened in disbelief. Kristen Brown was the biggest tomboy on the block! Markie Mandel had to find secret ways to escape the building before school so Kristen wouldn't challenge him to arm-wrestle and embarrass him in front of all his friends.

"Well, I suppose people *can* change," Kristen's father said late that night as Kristen and Prima eavesdropped from behind the door. "Maybe she's getting a little more feminine. She's always loved her pretty bedroom."

"High time!" said Antoinette. "George, that child is the least girlie girl I've ever seen!"

"Maybe she just wants to be her own person," Kristen's dad suggested. "After all, if your mother is a beautiful swan, sometimes you feel like an ugly duckling. Maybe you *want* to feel like an ugly duckling!"

"Oh, pish-posh," Antoinette said. But she phoned

Bloomingdale's and ordered a handheld sewing machine and enough fabric to cover the whole Palladino Building!

Now Prima and Kristen were ready to begin making costumes for their most elaborate ballet of all—the one they would stage at the Ballet Jolie. Late into the night, Prima, whose little fingers were very adept at threading, helped Kristen sew tutus and romantic long dresses and tunics and puppets and curtains and a lovely green collar with bells for Meowsky—which he gnawed off within five minutes.

One morning Prima and Meowsky shared Kristen's little animal carrier as they traveled by bus to the Ballet Jolie. By now Meowsky had learned that he was still a very tiny cat, while Prima was a very grown-up mouse with very strong legs, who could leap to the top shelf in the pantry and knock down the Fishy Delites. In return, Meowsky could use his nose to open the lower cabinets, where the cookies and crackers were kept, for Prima to chow down. So the two of them had established a truce.

When they got to the Ballet Jolie, it seemed that a great deal had changed in the time since Prima had left her old home. She could see the dust and the many stitched-up holes in the purple velvet curtains that once had seemed so perfectly grand. And the backstage was not only dark, but dusty and even a bit dingy. It all looked . . . smaller, somehow. Both she and Meowsky sneezed at the same time and began to laugh.

"So this is the great Ballet Jolie," Meowsky sneered. "It's kind of a dump, huh?"

"I'm sure it's much nicer in *Brooklyn*!" Prima snapped.

"You two stop it or I'm going to take you both home," Kristen threatened. "I want to look at where our ballet is going to be so I can paint the backdrops, and Meowsky, remember, you only got to come so you could learn not to throw up in a cat carrier on the airplane! Not like you did in the car." As there is nothing a cat hates more than to be embarrassed, Meowsky fell silent.

But Prima did not.

"Now, don't you dare scare my family," Prima warned the kitten. "When I was a mouselet, we weren't even allowed to use the *c* word."

Prima climbed out of the pet carrier and down onto the piano keys. She gently began to tap out the notes of "*Clair de Lune*."

"Prima!" Mother cried, and came rushing out of the piano.

"My girl!" Father shouted, and then stopped. "That smell. What's in that bag?"

"Father, now don't get your whiskers in a twist," Prima said soothingly. "It's a . . . a little kitten!" Father leaped back into the nest. "Mother! Come and get ready to defend the mouselets—"

"Now, Father, you have to understand. In the big world, not every cat is evil. Meowsky here is just a little kitten. He's got a big mouth, but he's more yowl than bite. I promise."

"First it's humans, then *cats*!" Father shouted. "What will she do next?"

Mother Pianissima said gently, "Father, he doesn't seem to have done any harm to Prima. And she does know more about the big city out there than we do."

"There can't be much difference between city cats and barn cats," Father blustered. "Why, back in the milk barn in New Jersey—"

"Father, give him a chance," Mother urged. "After all, he is in a bag, and Kristen is right here."

Pavlova was already poking a feather through the mesh of the bag to tickle Meowsky's nose, and he was batting at the feather with his paws. Swannie hovered over her shoulder, and Meowsky tried to leap up and bat at him, too. Pavlova laughed. "Your kitty thinks Swannie is a toy," she said.

"Oh, he tries to jump up at butterflies all the time, but he never catches them," Prima said. "He really is sort of nice, Mother and Father. Notice I said 'sort of,' Meowsky."

While her parents watched Meowsky with wary eyes, Prima ventured into the old piano to meet her brand-new brothers and sisters: Balanchine, Baryshnikov, Berthe, Bathilde, Sleeping Beauty, and Ivan.

"Ivan?" asked Prima.

Her mother shrugged. "Twelve children, it gets a

little difficult to follow a theme." She sighed. But all the mouselets were beautiful, and Prima could practically hold all of them in her arms at once. Her parents even let Kristen hold tiny Ivan. Still, there was a very sad moment. Mother drew Prima aside and, with a comforting hug, told her that Madame Mousielle had gone to join her *cher* René among the stars. "We all feel such a terrible loss when we look up at the VIP box. There will never be another mouse like your grandmamma. At least she got to see your proud moment," Mother said as she held Prima close.

"I'll try always to make her proud," Prima promised. "In my heart."

"She already was proud of you," Mother said.

Pavlova, who was coming along with Kristen for a performance and a long visit, had already packed her matchbox with her best feathers in case she met any cute mouse boys. "Mama and Papa want me to marry Reuben Delicatessa," she confided to Prima. And of course, being a Trapper's daughter, she also packed her Defeater helmet. Carrying Swannie on her back, she climbed into the pet carrier with Meowsky, who showed his sharp teeth.

"Cut that out!" Prima told him, and Meowsky obeyed.

"Now say 'sorry,'" Prima ordered.

"Oh, shucks. Sorry," Meowsky said.

"You must be polite!" Prima added. "Didn't your mother teach you manners?"

"I'll have you know that cats are the most polite of all animals," Meowsky said. "Don't we wash our paws before every meal? I don't see you doing that, Miss Mousie-Puss, do I?"

"Mice are naturally clean," Prima and Pavlova said together.

"I have only two words to say to you," Meowsky purred. "Litter box."

That night Pavlova explored. She loved the castle, the refrigerator, the doll bed, the view of the treetops, and everything else about life in the penthouse. But after a few days, Estrella began noticing not only sprung mousetraps but moths around the apartment, and said aloud that she just might call an exterminator. Kristen had to tell Pavlova sadly that two mouse sisters was one too many, and Pavlova had to return to the piano.

That meant also returning to an arranged marriage with Reuben Delicatessa.

"My stage career is over," Pavlova told Prima sorrowfully as the two sisters said good-bye. "But it's not your fault, little sister."

"But I'll come to your wedding, just like I came to Paris's wedding," Prima promised.

"And we'll bring lovely costumes for all," Kristen added.

And so they did.

Pavlova gave one last, great performance with Prima in *Coppélia*, with the most gorgeous sets that Kristen ever painted, in front of a hundred mice. The next day, with her long, green gown from *Coppélia* around her shoulders and a large daisy on her lovely head, Pavlova married Reuben and prepared to take up residence in the wall of the apartment above the deli by the theater.

But on the way out of the delicatessen jukebox

where the reception was held, the Pianissimas and a group of Mezzanina and Snacketta cousins suddenly ran into a specter from their worst nightmares—the dreaded one-eyed fighter cat, Knockwurst!

"I heard there was a banquet going on in there," he growled softly, "and it turns out there was. A banquet for me!" But just as he gathered himself to spring on the terrified mice, a bristling ball of creamy fur and flying claws came hurtling out of nowhere, yowling and scratching like a demon, followed by a huge human girl in a soccer mask with a goalie glove on each hand.

Knockwurst jumped straight up with all four paws and disappeared like a gray streak deep into the kitchen, where he cowered under the freezer.

"Oh, Prima, thank goodness practice ended early!" Father Mouse stood up tall. "Kristen and . . ."

"Meowsky," purred the kitten.

"Meowsky," Father went on. "We may come from different species, but I respect courage wherever I see it. You have saved my children's lives, and I am in your debt."

"The way I figure it," Meowsky said modestly, "is you got to look out for your own in this world, even if your own is mice."

"And I would do anything to help you and Prima and Pavlova and even Swannie," Kristen pointed out.

"You, Kristen, are a credit to your species," Father Mouse replied.

And so it transpired that one night, a few weeks later, as Kristen was leaving the Ballet Jolie with Prima in her pocket and Meowsky on a rhinestone-studded leash he couldn't chew up ("I hate this," he'd told Prima earlier. "I look like a girl!" Prima told him, "On the contrary, you look like a gentleman!"), they found their path blocked by a great, gray, skulking shadow.

"Now I'll have that bite," snarled Knockwurst.

Just at that moment, Kristen tripped. She tripped over what looked like an ordinary cardboard box, but it was actually a cardboard box with two nasty, half-grown kittens inside—Knockwurst's little brothers, Salami and Pastrami. Kristen struggled to get up; however, not only was her lip bleeding from the fall, but Meowsky's leash was tangled around her ankles, pinning them as tightly as a pair of handcuffs.

"Now you see why these sissy clothes don't work!" Meowsky snarled as the three brothers leaped out, all claws and teeth.

The one thing they didn't count on was Prima, who leaped from Kristen's pocket with her grandest *jeté*, took the steps of the Ballet Jolie three at a time, and gave her shriekiest squeak.

Out on the street Kristen had broken free and rushed to protect her kitten, who was holding his own. She batted at Salami, Pastrami, and Knockwurst with the end of the leash and they shied away, but not before their claws had done some damage to poor Kristen's legs.

Then suddenly, all at once, Knockwurst and his crew were assailed by an army of mice with bottle caps on their heads, all poking at the feline legs and noses and tails with sharp-pointed cocktail swords. As shocked by the sight as by the pinpricks, Knockwurst and his brothers took off at a run while the mouse army laughed and called, "Fraidycats! Fraidycats!"

Father Pianissima bowed to his troops. "Well

done," he said, and, though a little nervous about the prospect, allowed Kristen to pick him up and shake his paw, and Meowsky to grin at him in a way Father found gratifying (if a little unsettling).

Knowing that this was Prima's last visit before she left for Europe and that he might not see again the child who had brought him so many adventures over her extraordinary life, Father held Prima close. "You are a Trapper's daughter, brave and bold, and a ballerina's daughter, gallant and graceful. Don't forget us, little one, for Mother and I grow older every day. Even as you travel over the ocean, a part of you will remain with us, in the old piano forever, at the Ballet Jolie."

Prima was so moved, she couldn't say a single word, and Prima was never at a loss for words. She held her father tightly and then kissed Mother, Pavlova, Reuben, Paris, Mo Si II, Prince Charmant, Prokofiev, Pan, and the mouselets Balanchine, Baryshnikov, Berthe, Bathilde, Sleeping Beauty, and Ivan, as well as all her cousins and aunts and uncles.

"I love you all," she said, "and the Ballet Jolie. I never thought I'd be so sad to leave a place I couldn't wait to leave when I was a child. How can anyone feel two ways at the same time?"

"That's what growing up is all about," Mother said.

And as she said that, it suddenly came to Prima: In Paris, she would see—no, she would *dance at*—the Ballet Français Minuscule, the very theater where her grandpère René had been a star even brighter than the glorious Madame Mousielle.

It was not only a dream.

It was, Prima realized, her destiny.

La Belle Prima under the Paris Moon

KRISTEN AND MEOWSKY were fast asleep most of the flight to Paris.

But Prima was raring to go. In fact, she'd been raring to go all night long; several people had felt what they *thought* was a soft corner of a furry blanket slip over their feet during the trip. Her only mishap was an accidental dive into the lavatory, but with her strong dancer's legs Prima was able to *ballon* back up onto the seat. Far in the back of the first-class cabin, Prima had met an animal in a velvet carry bag, a stuck-up little woofing puller that looked more like a butterfly than a four-legged creature.

"*Parlez-vous anglais?*" Prima asked politely, hoping the furry bundle spoke something besides French.

"Shut up or I'll start barking and wake the whole plane up. Why weren't you flushed out with the rest of the garbage at Kennedy?" answered the little thing.

"Well, if you speak English, would you like a bite of this tuna sandwich I got from the galley? I believe it's albacore," Prima offered politely (she'd developed a fine palate living with Kristen).

"I only eat what my mistress prepares with her own hands, and then only chicken, small bites, white meat . . . but you wouldn't know about that," replied the animal.

"You're a puller, aren't you?"

"A what?"

"A *puller*, one of those cats that pull people down Fifth Avenue so they can get from place to place?"

"I'm a dog, rat face, and what you seem to be describing, and not very well, are *people* walking *dogs*. I have a very famous dog walker, Julian. He walks all the movie stars' dogs. He takes me out three times a day, and only to the best dog runs."

"You need people to help you walk?" Prima asked.

"Get out of here, vermin! I'm warning you!"

"For your information, I'm not *vermin* of any kind. I'm a mouse dancer, a ballerina, whose family comes from Paris, and I'm on my way there with Antoinette Brown, the prima ballerina, and her daughter, my *best friend*, Kristen, and my pal, Meowsky, who's a cat and doesn't need *anyone* to help him walk. He doesn't leave big poop on the ground, either, the way *pullers* like you do!"

The papillon began to bark hysterically, and her owner, a large woman in a black turban, snapped for the flight attendant to bring her *petit chou* more water.

"Know what *petit chou* means?" Prima taunted the dog while hiding behind a flotation cushion. "It means 'cabbage face.' Boy, what a *nice* name!"

She left the papillon furiously yapping, waking passengers who grumbled, "Shut that dog up!" and made her way up to the seat of a little baby who was happily watching the morning star from the window as the plane began to descend.

"Hello, mousie girl," said the baby in baby language, which mice understand perfectly. "Going bye-bye?"

"Hi, cutie!" Prima said, and gave the baby a tiny tickle-lick on the ear. (When she awoke, the baby's mother was surprised to find her little girl enjoying the remnants of a tuna-salad sandwich.) Prima sneaked back to Meowsky's carrier through the opening Kristen had left for her, bringing him the last bite of tuna. "Come on, wake up, Mister Cat-tas-trophy! You're going to miss seeing Paris from the sky!"

"Whaaa? Where? Whaaa?" Meowsky whined, slurring his words, "Oh, it's you, mouse mouth. Uh, yeah, Pa-ree. Whoopee. But you might notice, I'm under the seat, sissy. I'm not going to be seeing nothing."

"There's a really lousy dog back there," Prima reported, sneaking a snack from the plastic sandwich bag of grapes and half-eaten chocolates she'd tugged all the way from the galley.

"Well, I was so knocked out by the vet's pill, I wouldn't have known if it was Clifford the Big Red Dog." Meowsky yawned. "In fact, I didn't know if I was in the sky or the city. I dreamed I was sleeping behind the boiler in Brooklyn, where we had our basket."

Prima jumped out of the cat carrier and climbed up onto Kristen's shoulder. "Wake up," she whispered in Kristen's ear. "We're almost in the magic place!" And with Kristen rubbing her eyes, they looked down together on the dawn as, one by one, the street lamps blinked out in the City of Lights. Kristen snatched up her backpack and the cat carrier as Prima slipped into her jacket pocket.

George and Antoinette gathered up their thirteen carry-on bags.

Once the family was comfortably installed at the Hotel Trianon, word of mouse began to spread that the granddaughter of Madame Mousielle of the Ballet Français Minuscule was in residence. Prima, however, just acted like an all-American mouse. She gobbled her way up one side of the Champs-Elysées and down the other, meeting every sort of cute French mousieur imaginable. She looked at the pretty human dresses displayed in the shop windows and wondered why mice didn't regularly wear clothes. She learned to speak a few more words of the human French language, including introducing herself: *"Je m'apelle Prima."* She went sightseeing with Kristen, but when they took the elevator up to the top of the Eiffel Tower, she felt so dizzy, they had to go right back down. "And I thought the Palladino was tall!" she whispered to Kristen before they fell asleep that night.

Every mouse at the hotel, of course, wanted to meet the pretty long-lashed mademouselle from America. One of the laundry mice who slept in the Trianon sheet closet told Prima that the rumor was going around that she had begun her own *petit rat.*

"Rat?" Prima asked the young Laundressa in shock. "I think you've got me confused with the wrong . . . um, phylum."

"No, no!" the little French mouse said. "That's simply what we call ballet schools in Paris!"

"Gee," Prima said, blushing a bit, "I don't have my own school. I'm not a *teacher*, only a dancer. But Kristen, my human, and I have our own theater!"

One night Meowsky slipped out the window of their hotel room and went on the prowl. He begged Prima not to tell Kristen, who would have a fit if she realized her kitten was out alone in a strange city, and said he'd be back soon. "I'm only going out for a snack," he insisted, "and maybe to see if there's some good cat musicians doing any yowling."

Poor Kristen, protesting, had to get all dressed up and watch her mother dance *Anna Karenina* at the Ballet Français. ("If I see this show one more time, *I'm* going to jump under a train!" she complained to Prima, who was looking forward to the evening herself.) While Kristen was trapped in the audience, Prima was free to explore the theater, and crept down to the costume shop, where to her great pride and bittersweet joy, she saw a tiny scratching that in the mouse language (which is universal for mice of all nations) meant "On this spot, the great René Mousielle took his final bow." But before she kneeled at her grandfather's memorial, Prima dashed out through a crack in the foundation and found a tiny primrose to lay on the spot. Then she hurried to the Ballet Français Minuscule, one of the finest of the French mouse ballets, which was housed behind the walls of the theater's main rehearsal room. A performance of the classic ballet *Le Spectre de la Rose,* choreographed by Prima's very own grandmamma, was about to begin.

As she watched the dancers, Prima realized how much more elegant were the positions of their paws and how much more delicately they stood *en pointe.* True, Prima could leap much higher than even the principal dancers of the Ballet Français Minuscule, but she did not have their poise.

After the ballet, when the French mouse dancers excitedly asked the granddaughter of René and Madame Mousielle to join them in dance, she declined politely. But she stayed up all night in front of the bathroom mirror practicing their paw positions until she had them just right. She wondered whether it might be possible for her to study ballet in the French fashion when she returned home.

The next morning, as she and Meowsky were stretching in bed in Kristen's largest suitcase, Prima told Meowsky about the ballet and asked what he'd done during the night. Meowsky stretched but said not a word.

"C'mon," Prima asked, "did you see the Eiffel

Tower?" Meowsky opened his pink mouth in a yawn and Prima spotted a tiny brown hair on his tongue. "Meowsky!" she cried. "You . . . ate a mouse! Don't bother to lie! How *could* you? Didn't you even think of me?"

Meowsky pleaded, "I thought it didn't matter if it was a foreigner!"

But Prima wouldn't speak to him for the rest of the day, and in the evening, Meowsky promised to stick to his kibble and leftover fish from the brimming Dumpsters behind the French restaurants.

The following day Prima nestled into the backpack with the special peephole Kristen had cut so her friend could see, while George and Antoinette took their daughter to tour museums, churches, and the Palais de Jocelyne. ("I could puke," Kristen told Prima. "If I see one more little cherub, I'm going to tear out my hair! Even ballet is better than this.")

But at that moment Prima heard something that made her so curious, she leaped from Kristen's backpack and went to investigate.

"Prima," Kristen called as her friend skittered down her leg, "don't you take off on me now!" She hurried after Prima. George and Antoinette were so busy admiring a thousand-cherub ceiling, they never noticed Kristen running off as quickly as her goalie's legs would carry her.

"Behind this mirror, Kristen, listen, can't you hear something strange?" Kristen put her ear against the mirror in the empty castle ballroom. "Can you move it?"

Kristen pushed, and there was a hole big enough for Kristen to squeeze through. Prima hopped in with no problem.

Behind the mirror they found a human-sized room, where a mother mouse was playing a tiny toy piano, while a boy mouse—a young adult, really, Prima's age—practiced his *glissades* in the middle of the space.

"*Mon Dieu!*" cried the mother mouse. "Run, darling, save yourself!"

"Wait!" Prima cried. "This is my human! She's a trusted one." The mouse mother took a deep, trembling breath. The son, who'd been ready to fight to protect his mother, dropped his paws.

"How do you do?" said Prima, politely extending a paw. "I'm Prima Pianissima, and this is Kristen Brown."

"Eh!" said the mother mouse. "We don't care so much to be polite to these visitors who don't ask to come in."

"Maman!" the young dancer called. "Please don't! This is Prima! René Mousielle's granddaughter! Did you not know?" To Prima he said, "Are you surprised we speak English? We learn from the American dancers we watch." Prima nodded and smiled.

"Prima?" asked the mother. "I did not know." Quickly she stood up from the piano and made a small bow.

"Yes," Kristen said proudly. "Yes, this is Prima!"

As for Prima, she was speechless. She forgot her manners and stared at the young dancer. This was simply the handsomest mouse Prima had ever seen. He was light gray and had the thickest fur and the brightest eyes. Prima's little knees quivered.

"I heard from the other dancers that you were in town," the boy said enthusiastically. "The magnificent

Prima, who jumps as high as the moon! I am your humble servant, Abélard Pianoforte, and this is my maman, Héloïse."

Prima curtseyed and asked Abélard, "Do you perform with the Ballet Français Minuscule?"

"I am the principal male dancer," Abélard said softly and humbly, "but I am only at the beginning of my career."

"That was you in *Le Spectre de la Rose*?" Prima cried. "I wouldn't have known you!"

"Costumes," said Abélard. "And I am not so grand—"

"He is always running off to play the football," his mother commented sharply.

"But I love soccer too!" Kristen cried, and the three of them spent the rest of the afternoon kicking a Ping-Pong ball around the hidden room, while Maman made tea in a thimble, set out croissant crumbs, and clucked in disapproval.

After they said their thank-yous, and just before Kristen lifted Prima into Kristen's backpack, Abélard pulled her aside. "Will you meet me this night after my performance of *The Firebird*, behind the old rose-bush by the gate of the palace?"

"A date?" Prima asked. "I've never been on a date!"

"Is this what you call it in the United States?"

"A boy and a girl talking under the stars, yes, that's what we call it!"

"Then it's a date!" said Abélard.

Trembling with excitement, Prima agreed.

That night, as she watched Kristen wash her face and put on her pajamas, Prima worked up her courage. "Kristen," she finally said, "you're still a child, but I am grown up. And I know you worry about me, but . . . tonight I'm going out. "

Kristen's lips were so covered with toothpaste, she looked as though she was foaming at the mouth. Prima laughed. Finally Kristen said, a little sadly, "I know you know the way to the theater, but let Meowsky carry you on his back, to keep you safe." Prima pretended to be looking out the window. "Yes, I know that Mister Meowsky has been sneaking out. And one more thing: I know that you have a crush on Abélard." Prima looked down at her paws. "I know,

Prima, and it's okay. Why, Pavlova probably already has babies! It's your time, Prima. Just make sure he loves you too. My mother says Frenchmen can be heartbreakers!" But Prima's heart was beating too quickly. It drowned out all Kristen's words. She had not felt this way about anyone since . . . well, since she had met Kristen.

That night Meowsky carried Prima to the Ballet Français, promising to pick her up and convey her to the palace after the ballet. "Mee," Prima said, "no more snacking on you-know-whats, right?"

"I'm sticking to rats, okay?" replied Meowsky, muttering, "These French mice are all skin and bones anyhow!"

As Prima watched, Abélard danced *The Firebird* with the ballerina everyone said was his true love, the fragile Mimiou. But after the curtain calls, Abélard invited Prima onstage and introduced her as the granddaughter of Madame Mousielle. Then Prima went out to meet Meowsky, while Abélard changed out of his costume.

Meowsky looked about five pounds heavier when

Prima climbed onto his back. "Been gorging yourself, have you . . . you . . . meathead?" she scolded him.

"One sewer rat!" Meowsky protested, and quickly changed the subject. "So, Mousie Whiskerella, should I take you to the palace to meet the handsome prince?"

"He is very handsome!" Prima sighed.

"Far as I know, one mouse looks just like another."

"Now, you stop that, Meowsky!" Prima snapped, then said, "When you are all grown up, and it won't be very long, I'll bet you find a femme feline who will make your own whiskers twitch!"

"Naah," Meowsky replied. "I just like living the high life with good old Kristen, thanks!"

"Meowsky," Prima told her friend seriously, "you don't need to wait for me. I can walk back to the hotel. It's not that far, and I can get in through the crack in the laundry room."

"Oh, boy!" Meowsky howled. "Out all night?"

"Well," Prima said, "mice *are* nocturnal."

"Tell that to Kristen," Meowsky warned her as he trotted off back to the hotel.

*   *   *

At the old gate the two mice shook hands and kissed on each cheek in the French way.

"Your love is very beautiful," Prima told Abélard. "And such a dancer!"

"She is not my love," Abélard said sadly. "She is my *maman*'s choice for me. She would see us partner for life. But I have my own ideas. I am what you Americans call a rebel. And I have found the love of my life."

"You have?" asked Prima.

"Yes, and if you will permit me to be so bold, it is you," said Abélard. "Prima," he continued, getting down on one knee, "both of us have given our lives to the dance. But we must have lives of our hearts too. A mouse's life below the stars is short. Because of that, we can learn and grow and even make up our minds much more quickly that humans can." He stood up and, without another word, gave Prima her first kiss. "I would like to ask your papa for your hand."

"But my papa lives far across the sea."

"This is no problem!" Abélard laughed. "In France we have the carrier pigeons. I can get a message to him in two days!"

"I've never felt this way," Prima said, confused. "I don't know what to do." She held Abélard's paw.

"Look up at the moon," Abélard said. "He will tell you."

And with Abélard softly whistling "*Clair de Lune*," they danced a *pas de deux* by the light of the great Parisian moon. Prima was glad she had practiced.

When Prima returned to her hotel at dawn, Kristen was waiting up.

"Prima! You must never do this again!" cried Kristen. "I thought you had been kidnapped! I thought you had been eaten up! I thought you were lost!"

"It's worse than that," Prima said, a tear on her cheek. "Kristen, I am in love."

Kristen began to cry too, and picked Prima up and held her against her cheek, stroking her small head just as she had that day so long ago on the piano keyboard at the Ballet Jolie. Then, even though she didn't mean to, Kristen began to cry very hard indeed. "If you . . . you stay here with Abélard, how will I do without you? I mean I have friends—and I even like Markie

Mandel now—but Prima, Prima, these past few months, you've been like that baby otter . . . even though you are just a mouse. . . ." Prima's mouth opened in surprise. "I mean, even though you *are* a mouse, you and your family, well, you're like the little sister I never had!" Prima's eyes brimmed with tears too, and she hugged Kristen's finger tightly.

"I don't want to leave you," she whispered.

"I know," Kristen sobbed. Finally, when she had composed herself, she said, "Prima, I understand what you told me. I'm still young, but in mouse time, you're a grown-up lady."

"And," Prima said, "like the song says, fish gotta swim, birds gotta fly, and mice . . ."

"I know," Kristen said. "My mom told me all about reproduction."

"But don't be so sad," Prima told her dearest friend. "You'll be back here in a year or so, when your mother has her next performance at the Ballet Français! And I'm sure that I can convince Abélard to come to the United States. Everyone wants to travel and see the world."

Kristen looked deep into Prima's eyes.

Even though she was only eleven years old, she knew that what Prima was saying might be only a dream, and that, a year from now, when Kristen would still be not quite old enough to wear lip gloss or pierced earrings, Prima might be . . . Prima could be . . . she couldn't even think of it.

Prima was thinking the same thing. Now that she knew how long her life might be, even if she lived to be as old as her grandmamma, she understood from things Meowsky had said that she might never see Kristen again.

But neither one of them could bear to speak the thoughts in the deepest parts of their souls.

"Prima, I want you to be the happiest mousie on earth," Kristen said. "But I also want you to promise to never, ever forget me."

"Why, Kristen, I could never forget you! You're my friend. You're my best, best friend. You'll always be in my heart."

"And when you look up at the moon at night, remember, I'll be looking out the window at the

Palladino Building at the very same moon."

"And you'll still have Meowsky," Prima comforted Kristen as Meowsky crept into the room, silent as a mist, and curled up at Kristen's feet to overhear the conversation.

"You'll take good care of Kristen, won't you, Mee?" Prima asked.

"Never fear, mousie-puss," Meowsky said. "And I'll drop by and see the kids in the piano, don't you worry." Meowsky licked one paw and added, "Hey, I'll miss you, too, shortie."

"And you be a good cat, and stay out of fights, and don't eat any of my relatives."

"The way you mice go on, how will I be able to tell?" Meowsky said, but when Prima frowned, he assured her, "Don't worry, Prima. It's rats à la mode for *moi.*"

"You're a pal, Meowsky," Prima said. "I just don't know what I'll do without both of you. No mouse ever had such loyal friends."

"No friends ever knew such a mouse," Meowsky said, and he retracted his claws to pat Prima's tiny nose.

Prima Donna

ONE AND A half years later, Kristen did return to Paris with her mother, who was choreographing *The Sleeping Beauty.*

She was a very different girl from the one who had bid a sad good-bye to Prima and Abélard in the secret room behind the mirror at the Palais de Jocelyne. While holding a tiny white flower, she'd been the "human of honor" at Prima's wedding. She had taken many pictures to bring home to the Ballet Jolie.

Now Kristen was four inches taller. She was a seventh

grader who'd been to her first dance. She talked on the telephone so much with other boys and girls that she had to really concentrate to understand what Meowsky was saying anymore when he spoke to her in the cat language, but she loved him dearly just the same. She was the number-one goalie on the East Side Rockets and had startled her mother by beginning to take her own ballet dancing seriously. At Christmas she'd appeared as Clara in *The Nutcracker* at the Ballet Jolie—not because she was Antoinette Brown's daughter, but because she deserved the role.

And on the final night of the performance, she heard a strange squeaking under all the applause, and there were some of the nieces and nephews of Prima, with all their own children, jumping up and down on the old piano and clapping like mad.

As soon as the plane landed in Paris, Kristen called her girlfriends back home, who, of course, were all awake, because it was the middle of the night. She wanted to check whether Kurt, the boy who was her crush, really *did* like the lifeguard at the city pool better than he liked Kristen. Then, with Meowsky trotting at her heels, she walked downstairs to find Estrella (who'd finally agreed to come along on one of the Browns' many trips).

"There's a place I want to go," Kristen said softly, "but I don't want Mom and Dad to know about it."

Estrella stroked Kristen's curly hair. "The mousie?" she asked.

"You *knew*? All the time?"

"Not right at the beginning. But almost from the beginning," Estrella said.

"So why didn't you tell on me?"

"There are worse things than mice, especially pretty little mice who clean up after themselves, but I did think you needed another pet too," said the housekeeper.

"Why?"

"Just for the reason you're taking this little trip right now, to look for an old friend who might not remember you, or who might not be there."

So together, Estrella and Kristen, with Meowsky on his hated rhinestone leash, took a taxi to the gates of the Palais de Jocelyne. They bought their tickets for the tour. But quickly they wandered away from the guided tour and made their way to the little room all covered with mirrors that Kristen remembered. With a trembling heart, Kristen moved one of the gilded mirrors aside and peeked through the hole into the room between the thick walls. There was the tiny antique toy piano. There were the books on which the mice sat. There was the little ballet *barre*, made of bits of fence post.

But there were no mice in sight.

"Lemme have a look," Meowsky said. "If there's any mice in there, I'll find 'em soon enough." But he spoke so quickly, all Kristen understood was a sharp meow, and she was annoyed that her cat jumped out of her arms and shot through the hole.

"Meowsky," she whispered, afraid to attract the attention of the guards, "come back here."

Meowsky obediently leaped back into Kristen's arms, and gently they allowed the mirror to fall back into place.

Just then, however, they heard a noise. A sound so tiny it was almost like a flute, and almost like a memory. Estrella wasn't sure she heard anything. But Kristen knew it was *"Clair de Lune."*

She went running back to the mirror, scrambling through the hole, almost a little girl again who didn't care about scratching up her knees or tearing her fancy clothes, shouting, "Prima! Prima!" As she all but fell into the room between the walls, she saw the flick of a small gray tail. "Is it you, Prima?" she called more gently.

Slowly, slowly, ever so slowly, a tiny rosebud nose appeared, and two ears, and paws. *"Parlez-vous français?"* asked the little mouse. "I speak a little human English. I learn from *Maman*."

"No," said Kristen.

"Is okay," said the mouse. "I am half American."

"And what is your name?"

"Prima Donna," said the little mouse, stretching out one long, strong, perfectly extended leg and lapsing back into Mouse. "I am a teacher at the

Petits Rats du Ballet Français Minuscule."

"And your . . . your *maman*?"

"My *maman* was the greatest of all the dancers, an American who came across the sea to marry my papa."

"I see," Kristen said, kneeling down.

"My *maman* is naughty," the little mouse laughed. "Once, she goes on the stage with the human people all dressed as swans, and the conductor sees her and he begins to wave his baton so fast to shoo her away that all the swans dance *tooooo* fast and their feathers start to fly all over, and one almost falls into the orchestra."

"That sounds like her," Kristen said.

"And finally, for the Ballet Minuscule, she creates the most beautiful ballet of all, which is so very sad, *Le Ballet de la Princesse Kristeen.*"

"Who is Kristeen?"

"A princess!" the little mouse said indignantly. "A princess of America!"

Kristen sat down on the floor. "And where is *Maman* now?"

Prima Donna's eyes opened wide. "Why, she is gone now. To the stars." Kristen began to cry, and the

harder she tried to stop, the more tears came. Estrella, who didn't understand the words, did understand what had happened and put her arms around Kristen. "I am sorry," said the pretty mouse. "I miss her all the time *aussi*. Did you want to see her?"

"Very much," said Kristen. "Very much."

"But," the little ballerina explained, "she says I must keep studying and teaching the ballet, and I go home to that country, outside the walls, where my great-aunties live with my family, Pierrot and Pan and Palladino. . . ."

"Palladino?" Kristen asked.

"After the apartment building. And Pavlova and Jolie and Miau-Miau." Prima Donna dropped her voice and whispered, "I know this is a cat name. My *maman* once told me that there was a cat of the United States who was kind to mice. She tells me I must come once each week at this time to practice and to wait."

"And what are you waiting for?"

Prima Donna made a weary face and sighed elaborately. "I am named partly after my *maman*, and she used to say to me that someday the princess will come. And she will take me to America, to a castle high up in another castle. And I will be a dancer of America. Me, among all my brothers and sisters. Because I am Prima Donna."

"She told you that?"

"For this, *Maman* gave me a gift. She said, when she was old, I was to give it to the princess."

"Will you show it to me?"

"Maybe," said Prima Donna, eyeing Meowsky.

"It's okay. He is 'Miau-Miau'—Meowsky. He is a trusted one, and he does whatever I ask," Kristen promised.

So little Prima Donna ran to a tiny matchbox that lay on the floor behind the books. Very carefully she slid it open, and there lay a pair of peanut shells, tied together with a faded piece of pink ribbon. Kristen touched the tiny shells and remembered what Mother Pianissima had said, that crying for happiness and sadness together only meant that a girl was growing up. She laid her hand palm up on the floor.

"I am not very used to humans," said Prima Donna, shying away, her eyes wide.

"But I am the princess. I am Kristen."

"Ah," said the little mouse, "Kristeen. You sure are taking your time about getting here."

She nestled into Kristen's palm, curling her nose to her tail, and Kristen stroked her shiny gray head. "I have to pack before I go on the airplane," Prima Donna said. "I have many costumes. My *maman*'s. All made in America. All in a shoe box. And I must tell my *chères* aunties. And say good-bye to Pan and Palladino and Pavlova—"

"We have time for that," Kristen said. "We have all the time we need."

And so they took their time, and did all these things. And Prima Donna flew home with Kristen, teasing Meowsky all the way.

She became the principal ballerina of the Ballet Palladino and raised her children in the white grand piano Kristen got for her birthday. Antoinette never noticed, and Estrella pretended not to.

Kristen grew up. She moved the white piano into her own house and took a job painting beautiful sets for the Ballet Jolie. And though she could no longer understand the mouse language, she was careful to instruct her husband and then her children that they were never, ever, not under any circumstance, to set a mousetrap or chase a mouse out of Kristen's house.

They all thought this was a little funny, but they promised.

And years later, when she was a grandmother herself, she would fall asleep some nights on her sofa, near the grand piano, and listen to some soft, soft, ever-so-soft tip-tapping of the song "*Clair de Lune*" on the keyboard. On one such night, Anna Estrella, Kristen's little granddaughter, wandered into the room in her nightgown.

"What is that teeny song I heard?" she asked.

"Are you sure you heard something?" Kristen asked with a smile.

"I'm absolutely sure," said little Anna Estrella.

"Maybe it was a ghost!"

"Oh, Grandma!"

"Maybe it was a fairy!" Kristen teased.

"No, Grandma. Fairies are very quiet," the little girl said.

"Well, maybe it was a very special, very unusual kind of mouse, a dancing mouse," Kristen told the little girl.

"Like the ones I hear singing and whispering in the attic, in the old castle bed that was yours when you were little?" the little girl asked. "Is that why no one must ever shoo the mice away, even if they chew up a pillow?"

"Yes, that is why," said Kristen, pulling Anna Estrella onto her lap. "I'm so glad you can hear them. Now come. Let me tell you a story."

"About a mouse?" Anna Estrella asked.

"About a mouse, and a little girl, not much older than you are now, and about a great ballet dancer . . ."

"Do you mean Great-grandma? In the pictures on the wall?"

"No, a mouse dancer, who was also a great friend, very brave and very bossy, who loved chocolate, and who made all kinds of mischief but had such a loving heart, everyone always forgave her."

"That sounds like my kind of mousie," said Anna Estrella.

And Kristen said, "Mine too."